# DEFENDING KEIRNAN

## PJ FIALA

# DEDICATION

I've had so many wonderful people come into my life and I want you all to know how much I appreciate it. From each and every reader who takes the time out of their days to read my stories and leave reviews, thank you.
My beautiful, smart and fun Road Queens, who play games with me, post fun memes, keep the conversation rolling and help me create these captivating characters, places, businesses and more. Thank you ladies for your ideas, support and love. The following characters and places were created by:
Keirnan Vickers - Kim Ruiz
Dane Copeland - Terri Merkel and Yvonne T. Cruz
Dane's Military Specialty - Terri Merkel
Emersyn Copeland -Nikkita Marie Blake and Nancy Kehl described her.
Captain David Ferrance - Rosa McAnulty
Dane's siblings - 1 older brother Randy, 1 younger brother Ryan and a younger sister Rebecca - Donna Perry Byrd
Manny 'RipTide' Espinosa - Kim Kurtz

Maddox (maddog) Purcell - Rosa McAnulty
Beachwood Elementary - Kimberly Slorf Veihl
Beachwood Elementary Principal - Mr. Daniel J. Murphy
- Nikkita Marie Blake
Estella Copeland - April Shindlebower Brown
Robert "Auggie" Vickers. Auggie's specialty and
description - Kim Ruiz
Charles Watson - Kristi Hombs Kopydlowski and Mitchell
Maklin - Jo West And, Curtis Daniels - Denise Scott
Alexa (Lexi) Rodgers - Annette Reavis
Bekah Dodson - Michelle Eriksen
Harbor House - Michelle Eriksen
Jacob and Mandy Winslow, son-Brandon (Brand) - Kerry
Harteker
Richard Masters (father of Jax, Jake and Josh) - Christy
Seiple
Friday Harbor, North Carolina - Rhonda Rudd
Zane Hanson of Astec Enterprises - Jenn Hill
Curtis Daniels - Denise Scott

A special thank you to the team who makes it all possible.
Julie Collier, PA and Becky McGraw of Cover Me
Photography and Design for the amazing cover. It all
comes together because of these exceptional ladies.

Last but not least, my family for the love and sacrifices
they have made and continue to make to help me achieve
this dream, especially my husband and best friend, Gene.
Words can never express how much you mean to me.

To our veterans and current serving members of our
armed forces, police and fire departments, thank you

ladies and gentlemen for your hard work and sacrifices; it's with gratitude and thankfulness that I mention you in this forward.

# COPYRIGHT

Printed in the United States of America

First published 2020

Fiala, PJ

Defending Keirnan / PJ Fiala

p. cm.

1. Romance—Fiction. 2. Romance—Suspense. 3. Romance - Military

I. Title – Defending Keirnan

ISBN: 978-1-942618-51-5

# DEFENDING KEIRNAN

**When Dane Copeland struggles to rescue the one woman who can make his life complete, time becomes his new enemy.**

All Keirnan Vickers had ever wanted was to be a teacher. Having realized that dream, she's focusing on helping the local library with desperately needed repairs, so she has a place to host her growing reading program. Just when her life is beginning to look like a storybook, an enemy of her father's threatens her very existence.

Single father Dane Copeland has known his share of heartaches. He put love on the back burner to finish his career as a special operative with the Army and to raise his daughter. Fate intervenes when he meets Keirnan, who brings a new zest to his life and the promise of a new start. But it all comes crashing down when she is kidnapped and local law enforcement is unable, or unwilling, to undertake a rescue.

Partnering with Auggie Vickers, GHOST is born, and all of their lives are irreparably changed as the details behind Keirnan's abduction are revealed and time becomes their enemy.

\*\*\*

Let's stay in touch with each other. My newsletter (also called my Readers' Club) is the place to do that where algorithms, bots, and subjective rules don't apply. PJ Fiala's Readers' Club

# 1

———

Turning the corner and entering the back section of the library, which was closed off to the general public, Keirnan frowned at the condition of this part of the gorgeous historical building downtown. She'd been organizing the program, *Read with Your Littles*, for well over two years. At first it was difficult getting busy parents to take another hour or more out of their already busy weeks to bring their little children to the program; but it became an occasion to spend time together reading and talking about the stories and enjoying each other's company.

But, her patience had paid off, and parents began pouring in. There were children with a single parent; some parents worked long or odd hours. So, she had encouraged not only parents but grandparents to join in, even babysitters. Low and behold, her small project, *Read with Your Littles*, began filling up. They'd grown to capacity at the Beachwood Elementary School library. So, after only one year, she'd received permission from the Friday Harbor Town Council to move the venue to the downtown library. As generous as it was that the town had been eager to accept Keirnan Vickers' program, this old library building was in poor shape.

Many windows had been painted closed, which was a safety hazard. The handrails on the steps were loose, the flooring was sadly neglected and the plumbing, well the plumbing, was atrocious. That's when she knew she had to do something. The town had agreed to pay the lion's share of the repairs, but Keirnan had to initially raise donations to cover the first one quarter of the $500,000 repair costs.

With the help of her best friend and fellow teacher, Lexi, she organized a huge fundraiser to the detriment of her sleep. Did she invite the right people? Would they come with money, credit cards or checkbooks in hand to donate? Would the library be able to make many of the necessary repairs? Or would she look the fool? It was the last one that kept her awake into the wee hours of the morning.

Hearing a loud bang, she stopped and turned. Waiting to hear more or someone moving around, she hesitated to go investigate. The library was open now, but this wing was not. She was simply keeping her decorating stash here so she could bring it in small batches and not have to haul in carload after carload.

Another bang had her heart racing and the tiny hairs on the back of her neck prickling. Inhaling deeply, she slowly walked down the hallway and in the direction of the noises.

"Hello?" Waiting for a response, she could only hear her heartbeat thrumming in her ears. Swallowing, she called a bit louder. "Is anybody back here?"

Looking into the first room, grateful the sun was still

high in the sky, she didn't see anything but stacks of chairs on top of tables that had seen better days and bags of decorating supplies: pretty purple hanging decor, napkins, matching plastic wear and expensive looking, but not, plastic plates for guests at the fundraiser. She had wrestled with how fancy to make the event, opting for low budget, showing their future benefactors that they wouldn't be squandering their money on needless frilly things.

An old portrait of Mr. Vandebrooke, the founder of the town and this library, hung askew on the far wall. The eerie look on his face, that vacant look that signified the artist was not quite able to capture the soul of the man, just the body, gave her the chills. Did his eyes follow her? Shaking her head, she chastised herself for her overactive imagination.

Turning to the hallway once again, she ventured down it further to the next door. "Hello?"

From the corner of her left eye she thought she saw movement. Jumping and stifling a squeal, she looked to her left and surveyed the area. What did she just see? Nothing seemed out of place, then again, how would she know? She rarely came back this far other than to make lists of the things that needed upgrading. Another sound came from further down the hallway.

Her heartbeat pounded, and her hands began to shake. She'd never been one to scare easily, and she'd seen her share of old buildings in her twenty-five years; it was likely a mouse or a broken window allowing the breeze to move items on the wall or a door closing. She continued to the next room and jumped about a foot off the floor when she saw a man sitting in a chair in the far-left corner of the room. She'd never seen him before, not in town or in the library, but he seemed as if he were waiting for her to appear.

"Hello. May I ask what you're doing in this wing?" Proud her voice didn't shake proving her fright.

"I'm a potential investor in this great building and wanted to see for myself during the day just how bad the condition is."

Swallowing to moisten her dry throat she forced a smile. "Oh, I'm Keirnan Vickers, one of the fundraisers. I'm happy you've taken such an interest in the building and that you can see for yourself the poor condition it's in."

"Yes. That's clear as day."

"What is your name, please?" The way he stared at her made her skin crawl. The close to being a sneer on his face kept her from coming any further into the room.

"That's not important. I'll be on my way in just a moment."

"But, I don't think anyone is supposed to be in this area, Mr. ?"

"But then again, here you are as well." He stood and she guessed his height as just under six feet. His sandy-colored hair was slicked back, and tied together at his nape in a short ponytail. He wore a clean, dark blue, short-sleeved, three-button, placket shirt, jeans and sneakers. He didn't look like someone who had the money to invest, but a person could never know for sure.

"Yes, I'm storing some of the items for the fundraiser in this section to keep them out of the way."

His hands tucked into the front pockets of his jeans, he began walking around the room, first looking at the windows, then at a photograph on the wall. As he neared her, she straightened her back fighting the urge to turn and run. If he actually was a benefactor, it was imperative that she leave him with a positive impression.

"Well, I'll see you in two weeks at the fundraiser then, Mr.?"

He inhaled deeply, removed his hands from his front pockets, and looked toward the door as if ready to leave. She stepped aside and swallowed. Clutching her hands together in front of her, she hoped she didn't look as scared as she felt. His whole demeanor seemed bizarre at best.

He walked to the door, then stopped in the doorway, turning to look at her. His eyes stared into hers for a long moment before trailing down her body. The dreadful feeling that plummeted to the pit of her stomach left her ready to run screaming from the room.

He simply smiled, though it looked scornful. He nodded as if dismissing her and left the room.

Allowing herself a moment to regain her composure, and let her knees stop shaking, she inhaled and exhaled a few times, nodded her head and began walking as quickly as she could to the main area of the library to tell, Bekah Dodson, the curator, that someone was in the closed section. Her skin crawled again and she looked back and forth into the rooms to make sure he wasn't going to jump out at her or follow her. She scolded herself for being a scaredy-cat, but he was a creepy-ass man. The first thing she'd do is ask Lexi, if she had added to the guestlist.

## 2

___

Tucking his phone in his back pocket, Dane unlocked his gun safe, pulled out his 9mm, checked the clip for bullets, verified the safety was on, then he holstered his gun inside the back of his waistband. Closing his eyes for just a moment, he inhaled and let it out. He'd just gotten out of the service, after spending twenty years in, sixteen of those in Special Ops. Civilian life was an adjustment.

The past four years he'd adjusted a lot. First to losing his wife, Catherine, and being a single father to Emersyn, his smart, beautiful, funny, little five-year-old girl, with the help of his mother. She was a godsend. His father was gone, and his mother poured herself into helping him raise Emersyn. What would he have done without her? His missions were sporadic, and lasted for unknown periods of time; he would have had to leave his Special Ops Unit, which was his second family when Catherine died, had it not been for his mom. That would have made coping with her sudden death unbearable.

His phone rang and he dug it out of his pocket without looking at the screen. "Copeland."

His mother's laughing on the other end of the line caused his cheeks to burn red.

"I see you're still in the military in your head. It'll take a while."

"Yeah." Walking from his bedroom to the living room, he snagged his truck keys from the coffee table, headed to the front door and twisted the knob.

"Do you need directions to Emersyn's school? Are you sure you want to go pick her up?"

Stepping off his front porch, he chuckled. "I think I've got this, Mom. I know where the school is and after a couple of errands, I'll be on my way there."

"Okay." She sounded disappointed. Maybe sad. And he felt bad. It was an adjustment for her now, too.

"You could tell me which direction I go when I get to the school though."

The cheer in her voice was instant. "Oh, of course. Once you enter the front door, you'll need to check in at the office. It's on the right. Then, when you leave the office, head straight down the hallway, all the way down to the end, and make another right. Her classroom is the first door on the right. Ms. Vickers is her teacher. She's just the sweetest thing. Beautiful, great with the kids. Single, too."

"Okay, I get it. This is not a dating call, I'm not looking. I have enough to worry about after retiring from Special Ops and not knowing what I want to do next. I feel like a damned teenager again trying to decide what I want to do when I grow up."

"I know. I know. I just thought I'd throw that out there."

Climbing into his truck, he set his phone in the holder

on the dash, buckled his seat belt and turned the key in the ignition.

"So, Mom, I'll call you after I pick up Emersyn. Do you want to go out to dinner with us tonight? I didn't make supper but to be honest with you, I don't even know what to make. I feel lost in some ways."

He heard his mom sigh on the other end of the phone. "Let me make something here for you two. I was just feeling the same way. I don't know what to do with myself without Emersyn around the house. And, it's only been a day, but I already miss her."

"It's a deal, Mom. Emmy and I will be by around five-ish. Is that good?"

"Perfect. I'll make a roast."

"That sounds delicious."

Tapping the end call icon, he pulled his truck from the driveway, and headed down the road to the hardware store, then to Beachwood Elementary School.

Just making them dinner cheered his mom up. Simple pleasures for sure.

For the first time in a long time, he paid attention to Friday Harbor. The buildings were neatly kept, and while older, they seemed friendly and welcoming. Each business planted flowers, which would bloom soon; though the temperature was still only in the high 60's, it wouldn't be long before it was sweltering. North Carolina could get plenty warm. Catherine had insisted they buy a house here when he was stationed at the base in town and she found out she was pregnant. Sometimes military towns brought some of the seedier side of life, like tattoo parlors and the military whores looking for a lay or a husband. And Friday Harbor had that, but they'd purposely looked on the opposite side of town for a house and the instant they'd driven into the North side of Friday Harbor, they knew they'd make their home here. Now that he was out of the military and Catherine was gone, he and Emersyn could go anywhere. But, first he had to figure out what he wanted to do on a day to day basis. He'd saved money, not a ton but he was good for a while.

Pulling into the parking lot of Beachwood Elementary, he found a spot, exited his truck and walked into the front door. Everything inside was painted in bright primary colors. He checked in, received a lanyard with "Guest" typed on it, then headed down the hall. The school bell rang, and instantly, the halls flooded with kids of all ages. He dodged, moved, pivoted and generally tried not to get run over.

Turning right at the end of the hall, he found Ms. Vickers' room and stepped inside. Most of the kids were gone, only three remained and they stood at the back of the room looking into an aquarium. Glancing around he didn't see a teacher, so he walked to the back by the kids.

"Hey Emmy, what are you looking at?"

Emmy turned, her dark curls bouncing, and her big brown eyes shined with delight.

"Daddy, we're watching Thomas eat."

She tugged him by the hand to the aquarium, where inside he saw a turtle munching on some leaves.

"So, this is the famous Thomas I've been hearing about?"

The other two girls, one a redhead with freckles all over her face and the prettiest blue eyes smiled at him, and he couldn't help but smile back. The sweet little gal had a tooth missing in the front, but it didn't keep her from smiling. The other girl had sandy-blond hair and blue eyes and giggled, too. "He's really slow."

"I've heard that. Why is his name Thomas?"

Emmy giggled, "Daddy, it's from the book Adventures of Thomas Turtle."

"Hello, can I help you?"

He turned to see a beautiful young woman with sandy-blond hair and mesmerizing dark green eyes staring at him. Her face seemed familiar in some way, but he couldn't put two and two together. She was around 5'5" and slender .

Remembering his manners, he stepped forward and held his hand out. "I'm Dane Copeland, Emmy's dad."

The smile she bestowed on him was breathtaking. "Oh, it's so nice to meet you. I'm Keirnan Vickers. Usually Estella picks Emersyn up."

"Daddy's 'tired' now," Emersyn happily added.

He chuckled. "Retired. From Special Ops in the Army."

She shook hands with him and they locked eyes. His stomach flipped and he didn't want to let go. She pulled away first, after giving his hand a squeeze. "My father and brother are both in the military. My father is here on base, my brother is deployed to Bosnia right now."

"Who are your father and brother?"

She smiled. "Robert Vickers is my father and my brother is Gaige Vickers."

He nodded. "I know your father, just a bit, we called him Auggie. We worked on a few missions together. Smart, dependable, knows his job. I'm sorry to say I've never met your brother."

She giggled and it was like music. "Yep, that's my father. He's getting ready to retire next month."

"Dana, come on, honey." A woman called from the doorway and the little redhead ran toward her waving goodbye. "Bye, Ms. Vickers."

Her smile was infectious and genuine. "Good night, Dana, Ms. Shallow. I'll see you tomorrow."

Another woman stepped in. "I'm so sorry I'm late, Keirnan. Suzie, it's time to go, sweetie."

"No problem, Diane, I'll see you both tomorrow."

That left the three of them in the room and he just didn't want to leave.

The silence grew long, and he cleared his throat, "Emmy, let's get going, Gram's making supper for us."

"Yay." She jumped up and down and clapped her hands. She ran to Keirnan and hugged her legs. "Bye, Ms. Vickers. See you tomorrow."

He stepped forward and shook her hand once again, adding a bit of pressure and looking her in the eye. "Good night, Keirnan. I'll see you tomorrow."

Walking to her desk seemed to be a chore. Her hands shook and her knees felt weak.

"Holy hotness. Who was that hunk of a hunk?" Lexi asked as she sauntered into the room and half sat on the edge of the desk. Her blond curls were the perfect frame for her petite face. Sparkling blue eyes and a curvy shape Keirnan had envied forever. She felt like the scrawny too-tall girl no matter how old she became.

Blowing out a breath she said a bit dazed, "That is Dane Copeland, Emersyn's father." And he was hotness. Tall, dark hair and dark brown eyes. And, OMG dimples! She struggled to chat with him at all she was so awed by his presence.

Fanning herself with her hand, Lexi replied, "The widower you mean. Hot and single. Holy moly."

"Stop it. I can't get involved with him, he's the father of one of my students." But, boy if that weren't the case, she'd...

"You're nuts if you let that stop you. He's simply drool

worthy. And, school will be out in a couple of months and Emersyn won't be your student any longer." She clapped her hands together as if dusting them off. "Problem solved."

Laughing at her friend's exuberance, "What do you think John would say to hear you talk about another man like that?"

Leaning in closer, Lexi whispered, "If he saw that man there," pointing with her thumb over her shoulder, "he'd want him for himself."

That had her laughing out loud. "You're crazy." Standing and pleased that her knees had found their strength, she walked to the whiteboard and began erasing the last two letters of the alphabet she'd drawn earlier today. "Ready to go over the final preparations for the fundraiser?"

"Yep. Just let me get my notebook. Your place or mine?"

Giggling, "You can come back in here, the sun is so nice today."

"Okay." Lexi practically skipped out of the room. Her personality was so vivacious. When they first met, Lexi had made her laugh out loud during an all-district school meeting and they'd been inseparable since. That was four years ago now.

Bounding back into the room with a well-worn notebook, Lexi plopped it on a little table close to the window and opened it.

Grabbing her own, even more well-worn notebook, Keirnan sat next to her friend, the ridiculously tiny chairs they sat in at the small table only added to the fun of their planning meetings.

"First, did you add anyone to the guestlist?"

Tapping her pencil on her notebook, "Nope. If I knew the kind of people your parents had put us in contact with, I'd probably not be a teacher."

Looking at the names on the guestlist she either knew most of them or had looked them up on the internet, and the man she'd seen at the library was not on the guestlist. "You're sure?"

"I'm positive. I'd probably be a trophy wife."

Laughing at her silly friend, Keirnan said, "No, I mean sure about not inviting anyone?"

"Yes. Why do you ask?"

"When I dropped more items at the library yesterday, there was a man in the back area, which as you know is closed to the public, and he just about scared the bejesus out of me. But he said he was one of the potential investors in the library and wanted to come and see for himself its condition. The weird thing was he wouldn't give me his name and I don't recognize him from any of our research. And, he gave me the creeps."

"Did you tell Bekah? She knows everything that goes on there."

"No. When I left, she was busy helping some women with research and I didn't want to bother her. I hung around waiting for the man to come out of the back area, but he never did."

"Oooo, was he a ghost?"

"No. Gosh, Lexi, you just gave me goosebumps." She rubbed her arms with her hands to knock down the gooseflesh that had risen.

"You're the one always saying that picture of Vande-brooke creeps you out and you think his eyes move. Maybe it's just like a Harry Potter area back there and the pictures all move and there are ghosts and goblins. Maybe we should change the fundraiser to a haunted library thing and make people go back there in the dark."

Unable to stop her laughter, she nudged Lexi, "Stop it. I'm being serious."

"Me, too." Lexi looked at her notebook. "Can we get down to business? John will be home from work on time tonight, and well, I'd like to meet him at the door with nothing on."

Keirnan's cheeks burned and she could feel the heat climb up her body at the embarrassment her thoughts conjured. "Stop it. OMG, it's been so long for me. I can't believe it."

Lexi, her best friend, her confidant, and sometimes her tormentor with the sparkling blue eyes and curvy shape leaned in close and whispered, "Dane Copeland." Then she burst out laughing and the heat her body generated could have cooked supper.

Fanning herself with her notebook, she shook her head and tried, unsuccessfully, not to laugh with her friend.

Lexi shoved her shoulder with a soft push, then said, "Now, let's really get down to business. Did you contact the caterer?"

They worked for an hour, going over final details, and by the time they finished the sun had hidden itself behind the building and their beautiful sunny spot in the room had dimmed.

Hugging her friend goodbye, she strolled to her car, impressed that the temperature was still in the mid-sixties and her light sweater was sufficient to keep her from getting chilled. One stop at the grocery store to pick up the order she had placed on the internet during lunch and she was on her way home.

Her little, but neat and clean house, was on the same side of town as her parents, away from the seedy, icky side of town where all the whores hung out made her smile. Checking her mailbox without leaving her vehicle, she grabbed the few pieces of mail and a magazine from inside and drove into her garage.

Carrying her groceries into the kitchen, she sighed, as she usually did at being home. There's no place like home was so true. It felt calming and soothing after dealing with kids and fellow teachers, some great, some, well...

The newspaper she had taken from her front stoop this morning still laid on her counter and she flipped it open to scan the news. There on the front page was a large photograph of one of the library's major investors, Zane Hanson, standing in front of a building, which the article said he owned. The headline in bold, black letters said, 'Local resident, Zane Hanson, invests in Friday Harbor in a big way.

She started reading the article and it appeared that Mr. Hanson had begun investing millions of dollars in converting this old building into a weapons manufacturing business and factory. It was going to bring jobs, industry, new housing, more businesses, etc. A huge boon for Friday Harbor. The article continued that some citizens still were unhappy with the business of manufacturing of weapons coming to Friday Harbor. They had been outraged at the last Town Council Meeting when the Council voted to allow the building to be converted to a weapons manufacturing business and factory by Mr. Hanson. These disgruntled citizens continued to express their opinions.

Keirnan thought it was good news. Perhaps this would propel the investors to give more money for repairing and restoring the library in light of things progressing in town.

Maybe that man she saw at the library had something to do with Mr. Hanson's business.

## 4

"So, what did you think?" His mom asked across the dinner table.

"Of?"

"Dane, you know what I mean. What did you think of Keirnan?"

"Ms. Vickers, Gram." Emersyn reminded her.

His mom looked at Emersyn, a sweet smile on her face, and patted her hand on the table. "Yes, dear, I'm sorry. Ms. Vickers."

Then his mom, who clearly wanted to have this discussion, crossed her forearms on the table, looked straight into his eyes and raised her brows. No words just stared. Eyebrows up. That meant she was in it until he finally spoke to her about it. He could be stubborn, too. After all, she's where he got it from.

Inhaling a deep breath, he glanced at Emmy, who sat with maybe half her plate still covered in food; but she had her elbows on the table, and her sweet little face cradled in her hands watching them.

"I think she's nice. Dad did, too. He held her hand. Two times."

His mom laughed. "Oh. Well, don't you move fast?"

"No." Exasperation evident in his voice. If it wasn't, he was doing something wrong. "I didn't hold her hand, I shook her hand. There's a difference."

"Twice." His mother clucked.

"Yes, twice. Once when I first met her and once when I was leaving. What should I have done, dipped her and kissed her face off?"

Emmy's squeal of delight and her hands clapping was the instant he knew he shouldn't have said anything. It's just that his mom had been irritating the crap out of him since the second they walked in the door. And, truth be told, he didn't know what to say about Keirnan. Anything he did say would give her hope that they would get together. She was gorgeous. Yes, she was certainly that. Unbelievably stunning.

Was she sweet? Yes, of course she was sweet.

Was she good with the kids? It sure seemed as though she was. Emmy seemed to care for her a great deal.

He wasn't telling his mom any of that.

Rubbing his forehead, which was beginning to hurt, with his fingers, he again took a deep breath. Turning to his daughter he said, "No, Emmy. I didn't mean that. She's nice and pretty. But I wouldn't kiss her face off. I shouldn't have said that, okay?"

Emersyn giggled and his stomach flopped. Time to go home.

"Are you finished eating, Emmy?"

She held her hands up in front of her, turned them to and fro, signaling 'all done'.

Taking his plate to the kitchen, he rinsed and then set it in the dishwasher. Turning to grab Emmy's plate, his mother stopped him.

"I'm sorry, Dane," she whispered. "It's been four years since Catherine..." Turning her head back to see if Emmy was listening and, pleased that she'd run off to find her toys, she continued. "Catherine's gone, Dane. Let yourself love again."

Pulling his mom into his arms he hugged her. "I know, Mom and I promise, I'm not purposely avoiding it. I just haven't met the right person."

His mom hugged him back, and his heart felt a little lighter than moments ago. This woman had been his rock since Catherine passed. His whole life actually, but more so when his life had fallen apart.

She patted his back and gave him a motherly squeeze. "I love you, Dane. And Emmy, too. I just want you both to be happy."

Squeezing her back, "I love you, too. We're happy, Mom. There's all kinds of happy in the world, we're certainly happy enough for now."

His mom stood back, cupped his cheek with her right hand. "That is probably the saddest thing I've heard today."

Shaking his head, his mom turned and retreated to the table so she didn't have to hear anything he had to say. Coward.

"Emmy, baby, come on, we've got to get home and you've got to take a bath."

Emmy came running into the room, her dark curls bouncing, her shining brown eyes alight with her five-year-old fun. She ran to her grandma and jumped up for a hug. Squeezing with all her little arms had in them, she sweetly said, "Love you, Gram."

"Oh, I love you, too, Emmy. To the moon and back."

"No, Gram, to 'finity' and beyond."

His mom laughed and he couldn't help it. Emmy loved that movie and quoted it here and there, though not exactly correctly.

Hugging his mom, he kissed her cheek. "Thanks for dinner, Mom, it was great."

She harrumphed and he chuckled. Not getting into it again.

Taking Emmy's hand, he walked her to his truck, opened the back-passenger door and lifted her into her car seat. He buckled her in and walked around the front, and climbed up into the cab of his truck. Starting it up, he eased it from the driveway and headed toward home. He turned left at the end of the street and made another left to exit the neighborhood when he saw her. Keirnan. Talking to a neighbor on the sidewalk.

"There's Ms. Vickers." Emmy yelled from the backseat.

Almost as if Keirnan heard her, she looked up at him. At first she looked surprised, then the smile that lit up her face was like the sun rising again. The sweet little wave she gave them had his heart racing as if he'd just run a marathon. His throat dried and he managed a wave in return before he passed completely by.

He felt dazed for a moment, then stopped at the stop sign. Looking back at Emmy, he said, "Does Ms. Vickers live close to Gram?"

"Yeah. Sometimes when we go to the park, Ms. Vickers goes to the park, too. She said she likes the air."

He chuckled. "Does she have a little boy or girl?"

"No. She says not yet but hopefully someday."

Moving onto the next road and then one more he pulled into his driveway just a few minutes later. He'd clocked it once, he lived only 1.8 miles from his mom's house. It was perfect.

Then his mind quickly guessed that meant he was only around 1.4 miles from Keirnan's house.

---

## 5

The fluttering in her stomach caused her voice to quake a bit and her neighbor, Ms. Mullins, giggled. "He's such a handsome young man."

Swallowing to give herself time to calm down, she responded, "Oh, do you know him?"

Ms. Mullins, easily around sixty-five-years-old if not more, her gray hair cut in a cute, snappy style looked her in the eye. "I play cards with his mom, Estella. She keeps us in pictures of him and Emmy and not one of us minds when she pulls her phone out to show us another one."

This crazy reaction she had just by him driving past made her head spin. Could she still have teenage hormones running through her body at the age of twenty-five? That was dumb. She hadn't had a boyfriend since she'd graduated from college four years ago. She'd flung herself into finding the perfect teaching job and was so fortunate to have found one right in the same town her parents lived in. Then, throwing herself into teaching, she was doing a great job. Soon, she'd started her *Read with Your Littles* program and that took a lot of planning. At the end of a day, she just wanted to curl up on the sofa with a book, a glass of wine and soft music.

Now she felt sort of silly. She'd end up being one of those spinsters she'd read about when she was in high school. Never married, no children, lost in books and cats for the rest of her life.

"Did I lose you, Keirnan?" Ms. Mullins asked.

"Oh," shaking her head, "I'm sorry, I was just thinking about the fundraiser and some things I have to finish before the weekend."

Ms. Mullins giggled, then clucked her tongue. "Right. Well, you go get your things done, I'm going to see what Walter wants to do this evening. Good night, dear."

"Night. Hi to Mr. Mullins."

She absently watched as Ms. Mullins walked back to her house. But her mind was on someone else. She was going to need to get Dane Copeland out of her head and fast.

Entering her house, she flipped the television on to listen to the news while she made supper. Not caring for anything heavy, she opted for a salad, and a glass of wine. After all, why not?

Preparing and rinsing her lettuce she heard fire trucks flying past on the main road, just two blocks away. It sounded as if there were many of them speeding down the road, must be a big fire. That's when the newscaster stated, "Breaking news from Friday Harbor. The building located at on the corner of Chatham and Oak streets, just outside of Fort Bensley on Oak Street is on fire. Right now, it's contained to one portion of the building on the north side. Three fire departments have been called to keep the blaze under control as the building contains flammable materials. This building was recently purchased by Zane

Hanson, to convert into a weapons manufacturing business and factory. Mr. Hanson was unable to be reached for comment."

"Oh, no what a horrible thing to happen, just when the Town Council gave him permission to invest millions to convert the building to a weapons factory." She said to no one in particular.

Pulling her phone from her purse, she tapped on her mom's picture and walked to her sofa sitting to get comfortable while her mom's phone rang.

"Hi, honey."

"Mom, I just heard about the fire in that old building by the base. Is Dad there today? Have you heard from him?"

"He's there, but fine. He just called to tell me that he'll be a bit late as the traffic just outside of the gates is heavy so he's going to work a bit longer and wait for things to clear."

"Okay. I feel bad for Mr. Hanson. To feel as if there's a target on your back when he's trying to do something good for the town must be disappointing."

"Your father has spoken to him recently. He knew he'd be ruffling feathers, but is committed to bringing this business here. He's a big boy."

"Yeah."

She finished her conversation with her mom and stood to go finish making her salad when her phone rang. Seeing Bekah Dodson's picture on her screen she answered.

"Hi, Bekah. How can I help you?"

"Keirnan, I know you were in the back of the library yesterday, dropping some things off. Did anything seem out of place to you?"

"Yes, I'm so glad you called. When I went to the south wing, I heard a noise so I walked to the far back room and a man was sitting in the room, back against the wall, just like he was waiting for me to come in. It was the creepiest thing and he wouldn't tell me his name; he said he was a potential investor looking over the condition of the library."

"Well, he was moving things around back there. I found some tables moved, and a door to the bathroom in that wing blocked with a table. It also looked like one of the painted windows had been disturbed, like he was cutting away at the paint. But, I tried opening it and it wouldn't budge, so he wasn't successful."

Her stomach flopped, whatever he was doing there, it was no good. "Bekah, should you have the police go back there and investigate? What if he's hiding things back there, like drugs or something?"

"I don't want any bad publicity or any negative chattering around town before the fundraiser, Keirnan. No reason to keep anyone away that night. We need this money."

"We sure do, but I also don't want anything to be unsafe or anyone to get hurt. He was a scary man."

"I'll do a thorough walk-through tomorrow to make sure everything is put in place again, and we'll be right as rain for next Saturday."

The hairs on the back of her neck prickled, but there would be no budging Bekah. When her mind was made up, it was made up. Plus, she spent every day there, all day long, so if anyone would know if something was out of place, it would be she.

Laying her phone on the sofa, she finished preparing her salad, poured her glass of wine and sat to watch the news go back to regular programming, which was some mindless reality show where everyone backstabbed everyone else. Flipping through the channels, she found something less icky to watch, and pulled her book from the coffee table to read a few chapters before bed. She needed to get this strange feeling to go away before she went to bed, or she'd never get to sleep. Maybe thinking about Dane Copeland wasn't so bad after all.

## 6

"Okay, Princess, let's get rolling. Do you have your backpack?"

"Yeah." Emersyn sat on the floor in the kitchen, next to the closet where they kept shoes and jackets, and yawned. She didn't have her shoes on yet.

"Emmy, your socks don't match."

"I like these."

Pulling her shoes from the closet, he knelt down in front of her and slid her pink and white tennis shoes on, fastening the Velcro straps and smiling at his little girl when she looked into his eyes and smiled at him.

"Love you, Daddy."

His heart swelled. "I love you, too, Emmy." And suddenly he didn't feel so stressed about the time and getting her to school. Catherine would have loved watching her grow up. Her physical appearance was all him. But, her mannerisms caught him so off guard sometimes because they were so like Catherine.

"Okay, go get your hairbrush and I'll get your sweater."

"Gram braids my hair sometimes."

Father fail, he didn't know how to do her hair. "How about I ask Gram to show me how to do that, but today, how about a ponytail, I can do that."

"Ms. Vickers knows how to braid my hair. She can show you."

And there it was, that was Catherine. Coming up with an alternative solution to a problem.

"We'll see, Em. Go get your brush."

He stood as she skipped back to her bedroom to get her brush. He pulled her sweater from the closet and hung it on the doorknob. Moving to the kitchen, he wet the dish cloth resting on the edge of the sink, wiped the crumbs from breakfast into his hand and tossed them in the garbage disposal. Rinsed the cloth, refolded it, and laid it between the double stainless sinks.

Emmy came back into the kitchen, her precious face smiling, her brush and a hair tie in her hand. Smiling at her, he sat on a chair turned away from the kitchen table, and she turned to stand with her back in front of him. He gently brushed through her hair, gathering it in his hand at the crown of her head. She stood still as could be and let him take care of her hair.

Wrapping the band around her pretty dark hair, he gave the tail another brush, smiled as it naturally coiled together and rested against her back, and leaning in kissed her cheek. Her cute little giggle could heal the biggest hurts.

Handing her the brush she took off running to her room without being told and he admired what a great little girl she was. She came running back to him, her energy and exuberance a marvel. "Can we go, now?"

"Yes, let's go. Grab your backpack."

Picking her sweater off the doorknob, he helped her

pull it over her arms; she grabbed her backpack propped against the wall opposite the door and off they went.

This was the first time they were going into school together; his mom had always taken care of this. He was usually on base or on a mission by this time of the morning.

Relief set in when he was able to pull into the parking lot without waiting and found a spot not far from the door. The weather was still mild, so the distance wasn't an issue. Parking, unbuckling and creating their new routine he paid attention to everything around them. Other parents, what they drove, what they looked like, he was virtually a stranger here. But, not anymore, though he had no hope or desire to get to know anyone else, he did want to be aware of their surroundings. The world was changing, and he'd seen the worst of the worst in his time as a Special Ops soldier.

He held Emmy's hand as they crossed the parking lot, and into the school. A monitor greeted them just inside the door, taking names and offering the guest badges to parents, even if only there for a drop off. He slipped the lanyard over his head and let it drop to his chest before taking Emmy's hand again and heading to her room. He'd made it a point to get to school a little early today not wanting Emmy to feel rushed and then drop and run out on her, but as they neared her room, he wondered if that were the only reason.

Turning the corner at the end of the hall his stomach quivered a bit and he swallowed a lump that instantly formed. The door to the room was open and he could hear Keirnan talking to someone inside. The instant they stepped into the room, her eyes found his. Emmy ran off to hang her backpack and join a couple of kids in the back of the room looking at Thomas. His first thought was that Keirnan looked gorgeous today. Fresh faced, flawless skin and her smile was like a spotlight, the whole room lit up. Her clear, dark green eyes crinkled at the corners just a smidge and her full lips shined where the overhead lights touched them.

Shaking himself from his stupor he cleared his throat, "Morning."

He ventured further into the room and she stepped closer to him. "Good morning. It's nice to see you dropping Emersyn off."

"Yes, well, we're trying to form a new routine now that I'm home. Once I begin working, I don't know what will transpire."

"Oh, where will you be working?"

He felt that familiar heat crawl up his chest when asked what he was going to do when he retired from the military, because it was embarrassing not to know. Shaking his head, he responded, "I honestly don't know yet, I'm considering my options."

Her face lit up. "That's fantastic. A new start!" She genuinely sounded pleased, and again that mega-watt smile. Then as if a mind of their own, he opened his mouth and words flew out, "Would you consider having dinner with me?"

Her eyes grew round and she swallowed as her hands touched her stomach as if it had just lurched. His face grew hot because, first of all, what the hell? Second of all, well, what the hell?

"I'd love to." Her voice was low but her eyes locked on his.

He smiled at her then, for real, "How about on Saturday? Was that your house I saw you outside of last night?"

She giggled, "Yes and I might add Ms. Mullins is very taken with you."

He rubbed the back of his neck as embarrassment once again flooded his face. "My mom's friends seem to have taken an interest in us." He glanced at Emmy and Keirnan looked over at her, a soft smile on her face.

"Well, you're both attractive and interesting. They have great taste."

He watched with interest as her cheeks brightened.

"Ms. Vickers, we got a puppy last night." A little boy squealed as he ran to her, his frazzled, tired looking mom behind him.

Keirnan turned to greet them and he walked back to Emmy to give her a hug. "See you after school, Emmy. Love you."

Her little arms wrapped around his neck, "Love you, Daddy."

He moved to exit the room, when the little boy's mom turned to leave. He stopped next to her and softly said, "7:00 on Saturday work for you?"

Nodding she giggled slightly, "Yes. I'm looking forward to it."

He nodded as well and left the room, feeling that the future was beginning to look brighter.

Handing his guest lanyard to the door monitor, he exited the building and his phone rang. Pulling it from his back pocket, he didn't recognize the number but answered anyway.

"Copeland."

"Mr. Copeland, my name is Zane Hanson and I've been given your name by Major Dalton White. I'd love to speak to you about a job opportunity."

## 7

"Okay, let's go outside for recess. Grab your coats or sweaters and if you brought a hat, please put it on." Keirnan escorted her kids to the wall that held the hooks for their coats, hats and backpacks and supervised each child pulling on their outerwear. This process took a few minutes, though not as long as when it was snowing and the added gloves or mittens and boots slowed the process down.

Once the children were ready, she waited at the door for them to line up in one row. They knew the routine by now. She pulled the white corded rope from the top shelf of her closet and stretched it out. The children grasped it, and held on, that was the rule and how they moved through school.

Looking down the row of sweet faces, she began escorting them out of the room and down the hall to the playground.

Walking down the hall, she smiled at the colorful pictures children had drawn hung on the walls. The school was such a happy place to be, full of color and light. The sounds of giggles and once in a while crying sounded throughout the building, and of course, teachers instructing the little ones on the lesson for the class.

Looking back often she checked to make sure no one had let go of the rope and everyone was accounted for. Happy that they'd made it to the playground door without incident, she smiled her brightest smile just before opening it. Once outside they dropped the rope and ran off to play on the various playground equipment or to take one of the many balls in the bin alongside the building to play with.

Now the sounds she heard were squealing, giggling, birds chirping and the occasional car driving past the building. It was lovely in so many ways.

"How are things going with the fundraiser, Keirnan?"

Turning to see Principal Daniel Murphy, standing next to her, looking over the children, the ever-present toothpick sticking out from the right side of his mouth, she nodded then turned to look at the children as well. That damned toothpick always irritated her, especially the way he chewed on it. Once she saw him pull it from his mouth and tuck it behind his ear and she cringed.

"Everything is going very well. I'm so thrilled with the invitees who have responded that they will be in attendance. I'm hopeful we'll raise enough to replace some of the windows and the flooring and maybe more."

His voice, while not deep for a man, certainly wasn't high pitched either; he'd learned to speak in a way that made it not that noticeable if you didn't think about it. "That's wonderful. I believe I told you my wife and I will be there."

"Yes, you did and thank you for your support."

He chuckled. "What you're doing is wonderful, Keirnan, you should be proud of yourself."

Her cheeks heated slightly and she ducked her head down. "Thank you."

They stood in silence for a moment then he said, "What do you think of the Town Council permitting an arms manufacturing company coming into the area?"

She shrugged, "It seems like a great idea for Friday Harbor Military personnel retiring or leaving the base who would be a perfect fit for the jobs it will offer keeping them in town. And, from what I read about Mr. Hanson, he seems very philanthropical, so it certainly can't hurt."

Principal Murphy was quiet for a long time. So long, in fact, she began to fidget with her fingers in her sweater.

"I don't think it's a great idea at all. We don't need weapons manufactured here."

"Don't you think they'll be manufactured regardless? Why not bring the jobs and industry here?"

"Not in that way. There are a thousand uses for that building, weapons aren't necessary."

Turning to face him, thoughts of her father, brother, Gaige, and her brother's best friend, Tate, flooded her mind. These men would need or want jobs there. "Is it any worse than the whorehouses and tattoo parlors we have flooding the East end of town?"

He turned and faced her before saying, "Those aren't necessary, either." Then he turned again and walked back into the building.

She swallowed a few times to moisten her throat and to settle down her anger. He didn't like the industry coming in, but he wasn't doing anything about bringing another industry in, either. Typical, complain about what's here but not offer any solutions to help move things in a different direction. It just made her so danged mad.

"Hey, what's got you steamed?" Lexi walked up to her from the other side of the playground.

"Principal Murphy and his small-minded ways."

"Ah, yeah, I saw him talking to you and could see the look on your face." She sighed, then nudged Keirnan's arm. Lowering her voice, she whispered, "Wanna bitch about it after work over wine?"

Laughing she couldn't resist, "Yes."

"Perfect. I'll come to your house, mine is a mess. But, I'll bring the wine."

They giggled and she was grateful, once again, that Lexi was her friend and knew her so well. They could also chat about her conversation with Bekah Dodson about the library and see if they could figure that one out.

The school bell rang, and the children lined up in front of her, their faces bright red from running and playing, their smiles contagious. They all looked sent from heaven.

"Everyone ready?" She stretched out the rope, waited as each child held fast to it, then with a wink at Lexi, she opened the door as Lexi held it for them, and led her charges back to her room. Up next? Reading time, then only a half hour and the children went home. All in all, it was a great day. She couldn't wait to tell Lexi that she had an upcoming date with Dane Copeland, she'd be positively giddy over that. Every time Keirnan thought about it, her stomach fluttered and her cheeks flushed. Then she remembered, she didn't ask where they were going. How would she dress? She wasn't good at that sort of stuff. Lexi would certainly have to help her out with all of this.

## 8

P  arking at a meter in downtown Chastain, one town over from Friday Harbor, Dane plugged a few coins into the meter and looked up at the large brick and glass building before him. Chastain wasn't as old of a town as Friday Harbor, and the older parts had all been raised years before and new buildings now stood in their place. It was downright progressive compared to Friday Harbor, but that was the charm of Friday Harbor.

Not sure what this job entailed, and not sure that he wanted it, Major White urged him to discuss it with Mr. Hanson; he'd known Major White was a very astute businessman, for a long time. That right there told Dane he needed to check this opportunity out.

Entering the high-rise, he walked to the colorful sign in the middle of the lobby; each floor and section of the building was color-coded to the business housed there. He found Astec Enterprises, which encompassed the entire upper floor, and proceeded to the elevators to his left.

The building gleamed as the sun shone into the tinted

windows and set the ultra-shiny floors alight. The walls were a mix of walnut panels and stainless looking material which offered a unique contrast. Warm and solid, cold and solid. Interesting. Stepping into the elevator with two other men, both of them in suits and ties, Dane thought of his tan khaki's, tan shoes to match, and a gray button up shirt, no tie. But after sixteen years of wearing a uniform, he wasn't excited to get back into one, even if it was called a suit.

The doors opened on the floor just below the upper level, and the two men exited without a word. He waited silently as the doors finally whispered closed and his mind went to Keirnan. She'd looked beautiful this morning when he'd dropped Emmy off at school. That smile of hers was a sight to behold. Trying to remember when he first met Auggie, he wondered why he never knew about Keirnan. Timing was everything and he wouldn't have been in a frame of mind to meet her any earlier than now, so it didn't really matter.

The elevator stopped, the doors silently opened, and he stepped out to a room that spoke of status and prestige. The thick carpets on the floor and immaculate furnishings in golds, bronzes and splashes of blue were stunning. The receptionist at the desk directly to his right smiled brightly, "Hello, welcome to Astec Enterprises. How may I be of assistance to you?"

He smiled in return and replied, "Dane Copeland to see Zane Hanson."

She looked at a computer screen in front of her, smiled and stood. "Please follow me."

Following her to the other end of the room, she held her hand out to the plush chairs of bronze, gold and blue. "Please take a seat, Mr. Copeland and I'll let Mr. Hanson know you're here. May I offer you coffee, water, tea, or soda?"

Smiling at her, he shook his head, "No, thank you, I'm just fine."

He sat and his first impression was correct, the chairs were plush, comfortable and expensive. The view from this vantage point was spectacular. Through the windows he could see the city below, alive and full of hustle and bustle. Cars, which looked like bugs from this vantage point, moved in and out of traffic, people, who looked much smaller, crossed the street at the change of the light, all of them in a hurry and he mused at where they'd be going at ten am.

"Mr. Copeland, do come in."

He turned to see a man, easily in his mid-fifties, graying at the temples of his light brown hair with silver threads in his full dusty brown mustache. His smile reached his eyes, his body was rounded from long hours sitting behind his computer, his hand held out to shake his.

Dane grabbed his hand in a firm grip and shook while looking him in the eye. "It's a pleasure, Mr. Hanson."

"Zane is fine."

Zane turned and held the door to the back-office area for him. The moment he entered the atmosphere changed. There was energy here, people hustling around, getting work done. Telephones rang, though it was more of a light beeping, fingers flying across keyboards created a hum of activity.

He followed Zane to another door, which was opened and apparently waiting for them. Walking into a conference room, there was a pitcher of ice water on the mahogany table, with two glasses next to it on coasters.

Two tablets, and two pens neatly placed before two of the ten or so chairs.

Zane closed the door before motioning for him to sit at the side while he took the head of the table which was expected.

Without asking, Zane poured two glasses of water, set them again on the coasters, then folded his hands in front of him. The faint smell of smoke wafted around the room, but otherwise everything was plush and clean in this room just as in the waiting area.

"Let me begin by saying that Major White speaks highly of you. We've been golf buddies for more than ten years now. And when I told him I was looking for someone to run the test room for my new arms manufacturing company without hesitation he mentioned you. "

He wasn't surprised that the Major recommended him, but without hesitation was humbling. "Thank you. I've also known the Major for a few years, though not socially and it's an honor that he speaks so highly of me."

"He doesn't speak of many with such high regard."

Unfolding his hands, Zane started speaking and the excitement level in the room rose by one hundred percent. "I'm about practically bursting with enthusiasm about this venture. I've studied armories and arms manufacturing; I've been a gunsmith for years, and I'm an avid shooter and a gun advocate. I believe in safe handling of firearms, training and education. The guns we'll be building will be without a doubt, the best on the market. Lightweight, accurate, and a kick to handle. I'm expecting to wrap up a deal with the military soon to buy from me, which, of course, will cement Astec Enterprises here and help us grow by leaps and bounds. Despite the ne'er-do-wells in the town."

"Was that your building I heard about on the news last night?"

"Yes. Not everyone was happy with the Town Council's decision permitting Astec Enterprises to convert the building to a weapons manufacturing business and factory. Some protestor decided to throw a Molotov cocktail into a window, and it caught a small part of the building on fire. Luckily, the fire only caught in a corner of one of the main rooms. Mostly dust, some old papers and debris and not much else. Some of the rafters will need to be replaced, and a couple of the windowsills. It could have been so much worse."

Nodding, he continued to assess this man, he didn't seem twitchy or nervous but confident and excited about his new business.

"So, tell me what you had in mind for me."

---

## 9

Smoothing down the front of her dress, her hand stopped at her tummy. It flipped around inside her every time she thought about going on a date with Dane. It had since he'd asked her out a couple of days ago. Butterflies flew around inside every time he walked into her classroom to either drop Emersyn off or pick her up. He was solicitous and made it a point to stop and converse. Yesterday, he mentioned that they'd be going to dinner at a place he liked but didn't get to enjoy all that often, Harbor House.

Lexi came over this morning and helped her pick out her outfit, then they'd gone off for pampering. Glancing at her shoes, her nose wrinkled. Black heels with a sparkly black heel. Her red toenails, courtesy of Lexi, peeked out from the peep toe. The contrast against the black was striking. She'd been excited when she and Lexi had gone for pedicures this morning. Lexi insisted on the color and Keirnan had giggled most of the day about how pretty her toes looked. Now though, she wondered if it was too much. What if he thought she looked trashy?

Her doorbell rang and time for errant thoughts to go away. Inhaling deeply, she walked down the hall from her bedroom to the living room. Letting her breath out and twisting the knob, she instantly smiled when she saw Dane standing at her door with the prettiest bouquet of red roses she'd ever seen.

"Hi. Those are simply gorgeous."

"Hi back. I was assured they were fresh and should last for days. You'll need to let me know if they don't."

She giggled as she gently took the flowers from his proffered hand and stepped back, "Please come in."

Inhaling the perfume of the roses she smiled, then looked up at Dane and noticed him watching her.

"I don't know why women always smell flowers."

"They smell fantastic. Didn't you smell them when you picked them up?"

He chuckled and shook his head, "Negative. Although my truck smells like roses now."

"Perfect." She closed the door then headed toward the kitchen. "Please make yourself comfortable, I'll just put these in water."

Gently laying the roses on the counter, she reached up above the stove to pull a vase from the cabinet.

"Let me help you," Dane said, his voice deep and sexy.

She stepped aside and let him easily pull the vase down and hand it to her.

"Thank you."

She could feel the fire in her cheeks and, well, lower. Much lower. The things he just did to her body without even trying boggled her mind.

Filling the vase half-full of cold water, she stopped up the sink and began filling it with lukewarm water as well. As the water ran, she opened the drawer where she kept miscellaneous items and pulled out a large pair of sheers.

A glance at Dane and she saw him casually leaning against her counter watching her. That amped up the fire spreading through her body.

"I can't help but think this must be rather boring for you."

"Not at all. I'm interested in what on earth you're doing, when dropping the roses in the vase was what I expected."

She replied, "Roses are special. My mother always told me that when you cut a rose, it's almost like the stem sucks in air, as if you saw something that surprised you." She mimicked sucking in air.

"So, you should only cut them under water, so they suck in moisture, which will keep the bottom of the stem from drying and sealing out water."

He nodded. "I never knew that."

"Look how smart you're getting just watching me take care of roses."

He laughed and it sounded wonderful. Genuine. Masculine.

"There are many who would say I could use some learning, so, this is good."

She continued cutting stems and removing a few leaves from the bottom of the roses then placing them in the vase while they talked.

"What did you do in the military?"

He took in a deep breath and crossed his arms in front of him. But, his stance was still casual. "Special Ops, which meant, I'd do a variety of things. I'm trained in everything from shooting, breaking and entering, take down, search and rescue. You name it. I'm trained for it."

"Except for taking care of roses."

He laughed. "I'm trained now."

Giggling she had to give him that.

"Do you mind telling me about Emersyn's mom?"

She stopped what she was doing to watch his face. His eyes bored into hers and she saw the sadness slip through them before leaving. "Her name was Catherine and she was special. She was warm, funny, caring and kind to others always."

"Is that where Emersyn gets it? She's always so kind to the other students. Especially those who have a hard time making friends."

"It is. She looks like me, but she is her mother's daughter."

"I'm sorry for your loss. I think I read that it was a car accident."

"Yes. She was hit by a drunk driver. She died instantly."

She reached over and laid her hand on his forearm, still crossed in front of him. "I'm sorry."

He took a deep breath and let it out, stood straighter and smiled softly. "Thank you. Honestly, thank you for getting that out in the open, it feels better for some reason."

"I'm sure it does. She was a huge part of your life and she bore you a beautiful, kind and loving daughter. I'd hate to have her be the elephant in the room."

Uncrossing his arms, he took her hand in his and gently squeezed. "I see you're kind as well." Then he bent over and kissed her fingers and doggone if that fire didn't roar to life with a vengeance.

Swallowing, she watched as his lips, so soft on her fingers, stretched into the most brilliant smile she'd ever seen. He released her hand and she wanted to grab his hand again and hold on tight. She felt a pull to this man. Something she'd never felt before and it was exciting and scary at the same time.

Carefully placing the last rose into the vase, she turned it to a fro, then smiled.

His smile was instant, "They look splendid. Shall we go to dinner?"

She smiled at him, this gallant man before her, "We shall."

Reaching into the sink, she pulled the stopper out allowing the water to drain, dried the sheers on a towel and put them away, then turned to face him.

"By the way, you look stunning, Keirnan, I'll be the envy of the restaurant."

The heat crawled up her body again, she could feel her chest flush and then her cheeks. "I think I'll be the one envied. Let's go and see."

He stepped aside to let her leave the room. As they walked toward the front door, his phone rang. She turned as he pulled it to his ear, a shrug of his shoulders as he said, "Copeland."

## 10

H e watched Keirnan stop and turn to look at him. The black dress she wore flowed down her slender body like liquid. It wasn't tight, but that was the appeal. It had movement to it, soft fabric that moved when she moved. Her smile dazzled him from the instant he'd walked into her home and still did. She stood patiently as he took this call.

"Dane, this is Zane Hanson. I know you haven't officially started working yet, but I have a bit of an issue I hoped you could help me with. Someone broke into the building and tried smashing the machine we brought in today. They didn't succeed. The noise alerted the workers in the other part of the building that something was going on and they stopped them."

"Did you catch them?"

"No, they took off running."

"Okay. What do you need me to do?"

"I need to secure the building and with your expertise in all things covert, I wondered if you'd mind having a look at the building to see how we can shore it up and better secure it."

His eyes caught hers. Dark green with flecks of brown and a deeper hazel ring around the iris stared back at him. "I'm actually on a date right now, Zane."

She shook her head and held up her hand to stop him. She mouthed, "It's okay if you're needed."

He reached out and wrapped his free hand around hers and squeezed.

"I'm sorry, Dane, I didn't realize."

"I'll see if I can stop by a bit later. Will you be there?"

"Yes, I've got to assess if there is any other damage and see what I can do here."

"Okay. I'll call later."

Tapping the icon to end his call, he smiled at Keirnan. "I've not even officially started this job and there's trouble."

"Oh, I can't wait to hear about the job and if we have to stop there first, I'll be fine. Honest."

"Are you sure? It shouldn't take long to go in and check out the situation. There's nothing I can do about the security tonight, but I can look at it and, in the morning, pull together a plan. It'll also make Zane feel better that I'm working on it."

"Zane? Zane Hanson?"

"Yes. Do you know him?"

She shrugged, her lips glistened where the sunlight shone through the open door.

"Of him. He's on our guestlist for the library fundraiser and I heard about the fire at his building a few nights ago."

Opening the door he stepped back to allow her to proceed him out, she turned and preceded him through it, then he held his hand out for her key to lock the deadbolt.

Twisting the key in the lock, he handed it to her, allowing his fingers to brush her palm. Walking down the sidewalk toward his truck, he was terribly proud of it today. The black beauty gleamed in the sunlight. The color matching rims with the sexy studs around the outer rims sparkled like diamonds.

"Yes, needless to say there is a group here in town that would prefer he not open his business. But, it's a great business, Keirnan and perfect for this town. With the base located here, there will be jobs as men and women leave the military but want to stay in town. They will already be trained on handling weapons and proper usage. It's perfect."

She giggled slightly and he realized his enthusiasm matched Zane's from a couple of days ago.

"I do happen to agree with you on that. Let's go look at the building then we can go eat. I'll get to see where you'll be working. You'll be able to show Zane you care and can then get your concerns off your mind."

Opening the door, he smiled when the running board dropped down for her. His smile faltered as she stepped into the truck and he caught a glimpse of the sparkly heel on her shoes, then the adorable red toenails that poked out of the toe of her shoes. Sexy. No doubt about it.

She settled herself on the seat and he closed her door. Taking a deep breath, he willed his body to settle down from the rev he just experienced.

Opening his door and climbing into the driver's seat, the lingering aroma of roses wafted out to him and the soft sweet smell that he'd begun to think of as Keirnan tantalized his nose.

"You smell fantastic" he blurted out.

She giggled. "Thank you. I know it might seem a bit

teenager-ish, but I just love the fragrance. It's Love's Baby Soft. I've used it since eighth grade when my mom bought me my first perfume."

Turning the key in the ignition, he managed to not sound gravely as his throat constricted at the thought of her spritzing perfume on her naked body. "It works."

Backing from the driveway he turned the truck in the direction of the Astec Enterprises' factory on the edge of town where the military base and his new place of employment were located.

"How is the fundraiser coming along?"

A white Lincoln slowed as it passed her house and Keirnan's head twisted to watch the car as it passed them.

"Is that someone you know?"

She slightly shook her head, then faced forward but her brows were pinched together.

"I don't know who that is, but I've been seeing that car drive past my place a couple of times a day and it always slows down."

Without saying another word, he swung his truck into a driveway, put it in reverse and backed out. Speeding up to catch the white car, it seemed to see his maneuver and sped up turning the first corner and leaving their line of vision.

Stopping in front of Keirnan's house, he lifted the lid on the console, pulled out a notepad and wrote down 6978I White Lincoln MKZ.

"How many times have you seen this car drive past your house?"

She stammered a bit, then looked down at the notepad he was writing on. "A few times. Maybe twice a day for about a week."

He wrote that down. "And you have no idea who it is

in there or why they or he slows down in front of your house?"

"No." Her voice was soft now, almost a whisper.

He looked up at her and saw her jaw tighten and her fingers fidgeted with each other in her lap.

"Have you told Auggie about this?"

"No."

"Anyone?"

"No."

Taking in a deep breath he sat back, making the effort to relax so Keirnan would relax.

"Hey."

She turned her head to look at him. He saw the worry mar her beautiful face and he was sorry to have reacted so suddenly.

"I'm sorry, Keirnan. It's not normal for a car, the same car, to slow down in front of the same house on a regular basis for a period of time unless they are casing the place."

She ran her hands up and down her arms as if suddenly chilled.

"That's frightening. Why would anyone be staking out my place?"

"Can you think of any reason, Keirnan? Anything that would make someone watch your place?"

"No." It came out as a whisper. He felt so bad for her, but he needed to find out who this was and how he was going to keep her safe.

## 11

————

The drive was fairly quiet. Wracking her brain to think of who or why someone would have an interest in her, she drew a blank. She lived a tranquil, peaceful, average life, family, friends, mostly Lexi, and work. Her fundraiser for the library.

"There was a man at the library last week." She blurted out.

Dane continued driving but a glance at him saw his jaw tighten as if he were grinding his teeth.

"Who was it?"

"I don't know. He was in the back area while I was storing supplies for the fundraiser. The area isn't open to the public. I wouldn't have known he was there if he hadn't made some noise. "

"And you have never seen him before?"

"Nope. And he wouldn't tell me who he was. He said he was a potential investor in the library, and he was checking out its condition. I tried a couple of times asking him his name, but he wouldn't say. Bekah, the library curator, asked me the next day if I knew what happened in the back because things had been moved around back there."

Dane turned into the parking lot of the Astec building and she saw three vehicles in the lot. A gorgeous white Escalade, and two pickup trucks.

Putting the truck into park, he turned and looked over at her. "Are you sure you don't mind me doing this? And, if you don't, do you want to come in?"

She smiled for the first time in about twenty minutes, since they'd seen the white Lincoln in front of her house. It felt good to smile again.

"No, I don't mind. And yes."

He nodded and unbuckled his seat belt. Opened his door and hopped out. She watched his handsome face as he walked around the front of the truck and her tummy flipped again at her good fortune to be with him tonight.

When he opened her door, she caught a whiff of his aftershave and her nipples pebbled. Was there anything about this man that didn't affect her?

Holding his hand out to help her down, she carefully stepped down making sure her heel and ball of her foot landed firmly on the running board. Her flowy black dress covered her knees, not that she was prudish, but she sure wanted to make the right impression. Classy, casual-ish, but wantable.

Placing her hand in his, he squeezed and her heart beat faster. After she stepped down, he closed the door, pushed a button on his key fob locking the doors, then pocketed his keys. Taking her hand in his, he turned them toward the building and those butterflies took flight in her tummy. Too early to say best date ever, but, so far, it checked all her boxes.

Opening the door off to the left side of what looked

to be the main entrance, she stepped through before him at his tug on her hand. The room was lit by overhead lights, and some light streamed in through the dirty windows. The odor of the recent fire still hung in the air. This room was large and open to what looked to be the back of the building, since the windows allowed the waning sun to shine in, even though the windows had soot on them. Dust particles floated in the air before them and she tried not to cringe at what that might do to her dress.

Glancing at Dane, she noticed he wore black dress slacks and a tan dress shirt, no tie. He'd be handsome in anything he wore, which honestly wasn't fair, but he couldn't help it that he was dreamy. His dark hair still cut in a military length around the back and sides, though the top was beginning to grow longer, with a slight curl a bit like Emmy's, gave him that kept appearance, but those dark brown eyes, they were mesmerizing. Intense. Sexy.

"Dane, this is a nice surprise." A male voice bellowed out.

She turned to see a man walking toward them. His belly was rounded, his dusty brown hair and mustache neatly combed, his dress shirt tucked into expensive looking slacks which were smudged with dust and grime.

Dane reached forward and shook hands with this man, then quickly introduced her.

"Zane, this is Keirnan Vickers. Keirnan, this is Zane Hanson."

She shook his proffered hand and smiled at him. "Nice to meet you, Mr. Hanson, and thank you for accepting my invitation to the Library Fundraiser next weekend."

"Oh, that's why your name sounds familiar. I'm happy to help out. It's a fabulous cause."

He turned and looked across the room at a large machine that two men were working on.

"So, the vandals came in with large hammers and began beating that machine. We were able to fix it, so they didn't accomplish what they wanted, but still, we can't give them the opportunity to do anything like this again."

Dane turned and looked at the perimeter of the room, then at the machine. "What door did they come in?"

Zane pointed to the door on the opposite side of the room. "That one over there. It was locked, but they broke the handle with their hammers, then came in and began banging on the machine. Those two guys over there, were in the back of the building measuring for the next machine and heard the commotion. The vandals ran off as soon as these guys entered the room. I've called one of my maintenance guys to come and replace the handle, he'll be here soon."

"Okay, of course there's nothing to be done tonight, but I can figure something out for tomorrow. I have some friends that can set us up with security in a timely manner and, worst case scenario, we can get some local security guys to stand guard at night if you think we need it."

"I'd like someone here. If you have someone you can call, please do so. I'll pay top dollar to keep anything more from happening to my building. It won't take much more and folks in town will begin to worry about working at Astec because of all of the problems. I'd like to mitigate that as much as possible."

Dane nodded, then looked at her, "I'll just be a few minutes if you don't mind."

Shaking her head, she smiled at him, "Not at all, do what you need to do."

Pulling his phone from his back pocket, he walked

across the room as he tapped some icons on his phone. She listened halfway as he began talking to whomever he had called, and Zane turned to her and shrugged.

"Sorry to ruin your date."

"No worries, truly. We were on our way to dinner and this isn't an imposition at all. I figured Dane would worry about it until he could see what needed to be done, so this serves its purpose."

"You are very understanding, Keirnan. I appreciate it."

She hated to let her thoughts stray to the money, but honestly, if he appreciated her understanding, which she would have extended anyway, a sizable donation would be well worth a minor imposition on her date.

Now if she could get this creepy feeling about the person in the white Lincoln from crawling all over her skin.

## 12

Sitting across the table from Keirnan felt so right. She was an amazing woman. Smart. Check.
Kind. Check.
Beautiful. Check.

His breath caught a couple times during dinner as she talked about her *Read with Your Littles* program and how much it meant to her for parents to slow down and spend time with their children and share the love of books. Catherine would have loved that, too. In so many ways she was similar to Catherine and the things he so loved about her. But, she was Keirnan and he needed to remember that. He was so far out of his element here it was scary.

"Dinner was fantastic. I don't know why I've never been here before."

Her smile tended to make his heart beat a bit faster every time. It was no different this time.

"I'm glad I was able to bring you here for the first time. I'm friends with the owners, Jacob and Mandy Winslow. I served with their son, Brandon. They are salt of the earth people and I like bringing awareness of their restaurant. It doesn't hurt that the food is fantastic, and the service is outstanding."

"Dane, I heard you were here with a model and I had to come and see for myself."

Standing to greet his friend, Jacob, he shook his hand and hugged him briefly before turning and introducing him to Keirnan. Her cheeks were flushed bright pink at the praise; she radiated a warmth and freshness he hadn't known for so long.

"Dessert is on me. You pick whatever you like. Now I have to get back to the kitchen or Mandy will have me peeling potatoes for the next week. She runs a tight ship. Nice to meet you, Keirnan."

Winking at him, Jacob said, "Lucky bastard." Then turned and quickly headed back to the kitchen.

Sitting back down he reached across the table and took Keirnan's hand in his. "I am a lucky bastard."

She blushed again and bit her bottom lip, which, holy hell, did things to his body.

"Thank you." It was almost a whisper.

Giving her hand a squeeze, he said, "Do you know what you're having for dessert? And don't say nothing because I'll never hear the end of it."

She leaned forward and in an almost conspiratorial way said, "I can't resist chocolate. It's terrible and I'll likely be a big fat old lady because of it, but I just love it."

Laughing, he confessed, "I'm the same. I have a terrible sweet tooth and Mandy's triple chocolate cake is like a slice of heaven."

"Oh my God, that sounds fantastic."

He signaled the waiter, who came and took their dessert order. Pouring them each another glass of wine from the decanter on the table, he raised his glass and tapped hers against his. "To a lovely evening with a beautiful woman."

Her cheeks flushed again and he enjoyed watching the color blossom on her face.

The waiter brought their cake, took away dirty dishes and they began eating the delicious triple chocolate cake. Keirnan's hum of appreciation was like dessert on dessert. Great choice.

After a couple of bites, he said, "I'd like to take you back to your parents' house tonight, Keirnan. I don't like the fact that someone is watching your house. Leaving you there alone just doesn't sit right with me."

Setting her fork on the edge of her plate, she looked up at him, her full lips sucked between her teeth briefly before letting them out, then her tongue darted out and moistened them. If she only knew what that did to his lower regions, she wouldn't do it in public.

"Um, I don't know how to respond to that. I..."

"Let me try to explain it better. You've admitted that someone is driving past your house and slowing down twice a day. That isn't normal. Agreed?"

"Yes, but..."

"But, here's the selfish part. I'd bring you back to my house, but I have Emersyn, and it isn't right for her to see you spend the night, plus, well, we're not there yet..."

He felt like he was a sinking ship without a lifeboat. The look on her face nearly crushed him, it was a mix of sadness and fear.

"Emmy gets up early every morning and wants to play, and chat and eat, you get the point. If I lay awake all night because I'm worrying about you, Emmy and I are going to have a bad day tomorrow. Stay at your parents just tonight and tomorrow, I'll set up a security system at your place that will allow us both to sleep at night. It won't interfere with my security work for Astec and it's really no problem at all to set up."

She tucked a long strand of her sandy-blond hair behind her ear as she sat a bit taller in her chair. Swallowing a couple of times, he admired that she was taking her time in answering so she wasn't making a rash decision.

Finally she let out a long breath and said, "I suppose one night can't hurt."

Reaching across the table to take her hand once again he gently squeezed her fingers. "Thank you, Keirnan. I promise tomorrow Emmy and I will be to your parents' house in the morning to pick you up, then we'll go to breakfast; afterward, I'll set up a security system at your place. I've got what I need at home, so it shouldn't take long."

"You keep spare security systems at your place?"

Chuckling he replied, "Just one. I bought two of them when I set up the security at my house because I wasn't sure one would be enough. Turned out it was, and I kept this one rather than returning it. It's easy to use and easy to set up."

Relief flooded him when she smiled for the first time since he brought up the subject and he was able to take a deep breath

"Sounds like a plan then."

"Good. Now, did you want to finish your cake?"

"Do you think they'll mind if I take it home? It's delicious, but I'm stuffed."

Chuckling cause he felt the same, he shook his head, "They won't mind at all."

Motioning the waiter to bring them boxes, he pulled

his credit card from his wallet just as the waiter approached the table.

"Ready for your bill, Mr. Copeland?"

"Yes, we are Donny."

Donny pulled the book with the bill from his black apron and laid it on the table at Dane's left and boxed up their cakes. Dane lay his credit card in the book. Donny picked it up and said, "I'll be right back."

Dane stood, walked around the table and pulled Keirnan's chair away from the table. He hadn't had to act the gentleman in such a long time; it felt good to take care of a woman again. His date. This woman. All of it, it just felt good.

Donny came back with his card and the receipt, he signed quickly, and pocketed the receipt; he stepped back as Keirnan picked up her cake box, he picked up his and rested his other hand on her lower back as they walked to the door. Stepping in front of Keirnan to open the door, his eyes immediately landed on the white Lincoln exiting the parking lot and his stomach soured.

## 13

He froze as he opened the door and she bumped into him.

"I'm sorry, Dane."

Feeling clumsy and distracted she didn't notice what had halted him, she'd been looking at his, well, his ass. When he leaned forward to open the door, she thought she'd take a peek. After all, who would notice? Then. Bam. Just like an idiot she walked right into him.

"Hang back a minute, Keirnan."

His tone was a matter of fact and a bit demanding and more than anything it scared her. She looked at his posture as he let the door close; he stepped back out of the way of the door, his hand gently gripped her upper arm and pulled her back with him.

"What's wrong? What did you see?" Taking a deep breath, she let it out. Her knees began shaking and her neck stiffened with fear.

Dane turned and looked at her, his deep brown eyes, normally so sexy and friendly looked lethal, dangerous at first, then he looked into her eyes and took a deep breath then his face softened, letting his breath out slowly.

"I'm sorry if I frightened you. It wasn't my intention. But, I saw a white Lincoln leaving the parking lot. I couldn't see the plates, I'm not sure that it was the same car but just in case, I'd like to give the car time to leave the area."

"How would they know we were here?"

Her stomach began to twist and a knot formed in her chest causing her breathing to restrict.

"I don't know that they do. But, whoever it is in that car could have seen my truck leave your driveway and could be tracking us from a distance. It could just be a weird coincidence. I just don't want to take the chance."

"Excuse us." An elderly gentleman stopped and waited for them to scoot away from the door.

"Of course, I apologize." Dane responded.

Meanwhile she stood there like a deer with its eyes in the headlights. What on earth was going on here? Never in her life had she ever felt so vulnerable. And, kind of hunted in a way. And, helpless. That was the worst of all. Helpless.

Dane held the door for the elder couple, and she watched as his eyes surveyed the entire parking lot and beyond. He nodded to her and she stepped through the door he held open and into the parking lot. To say she was nervous would be tremendous understatement. Petrified was more like it. She still held her cake box like it was a lifeline even though she felt the heavy paper begin to compress under her fingers where she squeezed it. She watched where she was going, Dane alongside her, and focused on not decimating her cake box, 'cause the good Lord knew, she'd be eating that cake in a few minutes.

Maybe she'd have a glass of her dad's bourbon, too. For sure, she'd have a glass of bourbon. Maybe two.

Reaching Dane's truck he opened the door for her and they both watched as the floorboard lowered. He held her elbow as she stepped into the truck and the instant he closed the door, she let out a long-held breath and whispered, "It's going to be alright."

She watched Dane's handsome face as he walked around the front of the truck. He made it a point to look around them, and down the road just in case that man, person, people, whoever, was waiting for them. But, she felt secure with Dane. He'd likely been in situations like this before. He certainly seemed aware of everything around them.

Dane climbed into the truck and locked the doors. Inserting the key in the ignition, he started the truck then twisted in his seat so he was facing her.

"Hey, I'm so sorry for scaring you. This is new territory for me and I'd just rather be safe than sorry."

She smiled at his concern, feeling somewhat lighter now that some of the weight lifted from her shoulders. "I'd think this is just like another day for you."

His handsome head shook slightly. "I've never been involved with someone I care for who's in danger. Not that you're in danger, but there's something going on that we need to figure out. I'm going to talk to a friend in the morning to see if she can run the plates of that car for me."

"She?" It sounded jealous, she knew that, but for some reason that little green monster just cropped up from deep inside.

He chuckled then. "Yes. She. And someday I hope you'll meet her. She's a force to be reckoned with for certain." His fingers brushed along her jaw, the backs of them smoothing across her cheek. "I'm sorry our first date turned into a burglary, security set up, subterfuge mission. It should have been fun and lighthearted." He moved his hand to his right leg, which was bent at the knee and resting on the seat between them.

"Who says it has to be fun and lighthearted?"

"Isn't that what women want? Hearts and flowers and all things nice?"

Biting the inside of her cheek, she thought for a moment then replied. "My grandma always said to be careful about projecting what you want on others. What comes to you is meant to come to you and you need to deal with that fact to be happy." She picked up his hand, which still rested on his leg and squeezed it. "I have always believed that. Before our date tonight, I didn't expect anything in particular. I was excited to spend time with you. Nervous that I'd say something stupid and make you rethink your attraction to me. But, never did I make decisions in my mind on how tonight should go."

He leaned forward, his head dipped and his lips pressed against hers. It was spontaneous, soft, and...perfect. His full lips fit against hers like a glove fits a hand. When they moved against her lips, butterflies exploded in her tummy yet again and her heart raced like she just ran two miles. His left hand moved into her hair at her nape and held her lightly in place and she moaned. She moaned like it was her first kiss. But, it just happened.

His lips then nipped a few times at her lips, which sent vibrations all the way down...there. She felt moisture gather between her legs and her nipples pebbled and her fingers shook. He was wholly exciting.

"I've wanted to do that for a bit over a week now. It did not disappoint."

"No, it didn't."

He turned then and put his seat belt on. Looking over at her he smiled and it made her dizzy. Her hormones were a mess right now. "Buckle up, Princess."

She giggled at the term. "Princess?"

"Just now it seemed to fit for you."

And there it was. She felt like a princess. Her chariot was a pickup truck, although a nice one. Her handsome prince a badass special operative, newly retired, but still on duty. Life could be worse.

## 14

————

Sitting on the sofa in the Vickers' living room with a bourbon in his hand, Keirnan at his right, Auggie across the room on the loveseat with Keirnan's mom, Elaine and pictures all around this stately room of Keirnan and her brother, Gaige, it couldn't have felt more surreal. He pushed back the memories of meeting Catherine's parents for the first time, though the two scenarios seemed almost as if they were one. It didn't matter that he knew Auggie; he was at this house because he was on a date with Auggie's daughter.

"So, this car, you got the plates on it?" Auggie asked.

Bringing himself back to the present, he looked at Auggie. "I did." He pulled the sheet of paper from his pocket, opened it up on his leg, pulled his phone from his left pocket and snapped a picture of the note, then handed it to Auggie.

"I have a friend I was going to ask to run the plates in the morning, but if you have contacts who can get it done faster, I'd appreciate it. It would be a side job for Angie."

Auggie looked at the note he'd written and nodded his head. "I've got a contact. Give me a few minutes."

He left the room and entered his office which was across the foyer from the living room. His voice could be heard as he spoke to someone on the phone, but not the actual words. Though it didn't take a genius to figure out what he was saying.

Elaine leaned forward then, eagerness on her face and in her voice. "So how long have you two been dating?"

"Mom." Keirnan said in a warning tone, which only caused Elaine to smile at her daughter.

"A mom wants to know these things. You'll learn that one day."

Keirnan wrinkled her cute little nose, then said, "Did I tell either of you that more than seventy-two percent of the people I invited to the fundraiser have replied with a yes?"

Changing the subject, smart.

Auggie entered the room, clapped his hands together and announced, "We should have results in a few hours. Dane, thank you so much for thinking quickly and getting this information."

Dane smiled at him then, and replied, "I think Keirnan should stay here tonight. Since the person in that car seems so interested in her house, she shouldn't be there alone."

"I agree," Auggie exclaimed.

Keirnan set her glass of bourbon on the coffee table in front of her and said, "Should we call the police to drive by and watch it over night? If this person notices that I haven't come home, they might take that as a good time to go in and ransack or snoop. Which terrifies me, I'll never be able to sleep there again."

He turned to her, looking her in the eyes, the dark green orbs seemed to change color in this light and seemed a lighter shade of green. The thick lashes that framed them created the perfect outline for their almond shape. "I have to go pick up Emmy at my mom's house and she just lives a couple of streets over from you. I'll drive by and make sure it looks good on the way there and on the way home."

He turned to Elaine, "Emmy is my five-year-old daughter."

Keirnan reached for his hand, which gave him a thrill that she'd initiate a touch in front of her parents. She squeezed his hand then softly said, "But what about the rest of the night?"

What he wouldn't give to just say, "Let's go and stay there together. All night. Alone." Just the thought made his pants tighten to an uncomfortable degree.

"Do you want me to stay there? To make sure no one breaks in. Emmy can stay at Mom's tonight."

"No, I can't ask you to do that, but..." She cocked her head to the side and let out a breath. He saw it in her eyes when she changed her mind. "It's just stuff in there, really. Basically my notebooks with all of my fundraiser stuff. Everything else I can replace if something happens to it."

"Honey," Elaine said. "You're right, it is just stuff. But if it would make you feel better, your father can go over and get your notebooks and bring them back here. Then maybe you'll be able to get some sleep tonight."

Auggie responded first, "I can do that. Actually, Dane can come with me and watch for anything nefarious while I grab your notebooks. What else do you need from the house?"

"You could grab a pair of jeans from my closet and a t-shirt for tomorrow."

Auggie stood which told him it was time to go. Resisting the urge to salute him, Dane stood, walked to Elaine and held his hand out to shake hers. "Thank you for your hospitality, Mrs. Vickers."

She giggled and it sounded familiar. Keirnan sounded like her mom in that respect.

Auggie walked ahead of him saying over his shoulder, "I'll be in my truck and can follow you, Dane."

"Yes, sir." He replied without thinking. Keirnan came to stand beside him, took his hand once again and tugged him to the front door.

He opened the door and waited as she passed through first, then he followed close behind her. So sorry the date was already over and that it had taken this sort of turn. Next time, tomorrow, they'd spend more time getting to know each other.

On the front porch of the Vickers' home, he turned to face her, cupped her face between his hands and said, "I'll be here in the morning, around seven if that's okay with you, and take you and Emmy to breakfast. Then, we'll get things settled at your house with security and then maybe we can rectify this date with an afternoon at the zoo."

Her smile wiped away the darkness of the date. "I'd love that. All of it. Yes."

He leaned down, hesitated just a split second before touching his lips to hers. Softly, was all he meant to do. Who knew if Auggie was watching, then again, he didn't really care. Much. And the feel of Keirnan's lips against his made it all so worth it. Hers were soft, and the feeling of his lips against hers was like a little slice of heaven. When he moved his lips, she instantly moved hers, too, it was as if they were listening to the same music and dancing to the same song. In sync. Perfect unison.

The blood rushing through his body sped up, the pace his heart set caused his hands to shake slightly and his dress pants tightened. Tomorrow, he'd pull her into his arms and feel her body pressed against his. He'd be thinking about that as he fell asleep tonight. If he fell asleep. That was a big if.

## 15

Filling two travel tumblers with coffee, Keirnan fixed hers with a spoon of powdered creamer, stirred it, then pushed the lid on tight. Not sure how Dane liked his coffee, if he liked coffee, she simply put the lid on his cup for now. When he got here, she'd fix it up for him. She'd barely slept last night, thinking about him. Their date and, of course, the person in the white car.

Her father had said no one was lurking about and it didn't appear that anything was disturbed in her house, but he wasn't there on a daily basis, so she'd have to check that over this morning.

"I see you're up early," her father said as he entered the kitchen.

"Yes, Dane will be here in a few minutes. You want coffee, Dad?"

Her father smiled, walked to her and kissed her temple. "I would, sweetheart."

Pulling his favorite cup from the cupboard she smiled knowing he still used it every morning. She'd bought it for him for Father's Day, so many years ago, when she had gotten her first babysitting job and had her own money to spend. It was Army green and said, "Army Dad". He'd smiled and kissed her just like he did this morning, and said, "I'll use it every day."

Her brother Gaige was the one who spoiled it for her. "Keirnan, you're so stupid. Army dad means you have a kid in the Army. Dad doesn't have one in the Army. Yet. Not till I go in."

She looked over at her dad to see his reaction but he just smiled, and said, "It means whatever Keirnan wants it to mean, Gaige."

Then, to prove it to her, he got up, rinsed the cup out, poured the coffee he was drinking into this cup and proceeded to drink the rest of his coffee from this mug. He'd used it every day since that one. He always rinsed it when he was finished, dried it with a towel, and placed it back on the shelf for the next day.

She'd felt stupid that day. She was thirteen years old and had babysat the neighbor girl, Shelly, for three afternoons after school for that mug. When she went to school the next morning, she went to class early while all the other students were still in the common area, relieved that her teacher was in the classroom alone.

"Ms. Leonard?"

Ms. Leonard looked up from the papers she was grading, pulled her glasses from her face and smiled at her. "Yes, Keirnan, how can I help you?"

"I have a question."

"Okay, let me see if I can answer it for you."

Walking up to the big wooden desk, she swallowed and told Ms. Leonard about the mug and what Gaige had said.

Ms. Leonard smiled at her. "Brothers can really get your goat sometimes, can't they?" Tucking her dark-brown hair behind her ear, she continued, "I suspect your father is correct, it can mean whatever you want it to mean. What does it mean to you?"

"Well, my dad is in the Army and he's my dad."

"Yes, I think that's perfect."

The rest of the day she felt excited to get home and tell Gaige what Ms. Leonard said. She also knew she wanted to be a teacher someday so she could help another little girl with a dilemma such as this one.

Pouring her father's coffee into his well-worn mug, she heard Dane's truck pull into the driveway and butterflies soared in her tummy. Taking her father his black coffee, she exited the kitchen and walked to the front door just as Dane began to knock.

The look on his face caused her to giggle. "Good morning. Come on in."

"Were you standing there waiting? I'm not late, am I?"

"No, I heard your truck."

She stepped back as he entered the house, then so excited to touch him, she took his hand in hers and shivers ran up her arms. But that was nothing compared to the shockwaves that sizzled through her when he leaned down and kissed her.

"Good morning", his deep husky voice floated over her.

"Morning, she whispered, still trying to get her senses back.

"Do you like coffee?"

"Yes, black."

"Where's Emmy?"

"My mom kept her last night so I didn't have to wake

her to bring her home; so, when you're ready, we'll swing by my mom's to get her first before we go to breakfast."

"That's really nice of your mom to keep her."

"She misses her terribly, she's used to spending more time with Emmy, but now that I'm home, Emmy's with me unless there's a special reason."

Walking with him to the back of the house where her father still sat drinking his coffee and reading the morning paper, she allowed herself to dream that this could be her life. More accurately, that Dane could be in her life always.

"Dane, good morning. You're both off to an early start this morning."

"Yes, sir. I wanted the time to install the security system in Keirnan's house so we can have some fun this afternoon. We're taking Emmy to the zoo."

"Well, that sounds like a wonderful time." Her father responded.

"Any word on the license plate from your contact?"

Her father looked up from his newspaper and clamped his jaw. "It's from a rental company on the other side of the state. I'm trying to work with their local police to get information from the rental agency, but so far not having a lot of luck. I'm thinking of taking a drive this morning."

"Do you need assistance?"

"No, but thank you. I've got a contact on that side of the state I'm going to lean on first. If I get nowhere with him, then I'll be going myself. Sometimes I'm irritated with the red tape that surrounds things like this."

"I agree," Dane said, then looked over at her and winked.

Grabbing their coffees from the counter, she handed

Dane his, leaned over and kissed her father's temple and said, "Tell mom I'll call her later. Love you, Dad. Be careful."

"I love you, too, sweetheart. I will. You two just get your security system installed."

Dane stepped back for her to proceed him. She heard him say goodbye to her dad, but she was so excited to spend the day with him, she had to hold herself back from bolting out the door. Almost like when she was a teenager and had her first date. Leaving the same house. The more things changed, the more they stayed the same.

Dane, just like before, opened her door for her, and waited for her to get situated before closing her door. She inhaled the aroma of his truck which was a mix of leather and Dane's spicy aftershave. And it was delicious.

He opened his door and jumped up into the truck, put his key in the ignition and started it up. Fastening his seat belt, he chuckled. "Did your dad tell you he gave me the speech last night?"

Her head flopped back against the seat. "No, my God, how bad was it?"

Putting the truck in gear and backing out of her parents' driveway, he chuckled again. "Not as bad as I'll be when Emmy starts dating."

She giggled then. "I'm sorry."

"Don't be. It makes me respect him more. And, for the record, he said he was pleased that you were dating me. He seems to respect me. I respect him. It's all good."

"Okay." She looked out the window at the passing scenery. "You know, I don't feel like I'm in danger or anything. It seems as if someone were really after me, I'd have had more scary episodes or something. Is that wrong?"

"Victims don't always have warnings or signals before getting in trouble, Keirnan. And, you're fortunate in that we can make sure you're safe, and if it's nothing, then, all the better."

"Right."

"Now, tell me again about this guy you saw at the library."

# 16

---

Entering Keirnan's house for the third time in a twenty-four-hour period Dane felt oddly relaxed. He knew this feeling. There was really no denying it, he enjoyed Keirnan and wanted to spend time with her. It was a bonus that she knew Emersyn so well and they got along splendidly.

"Okay Emmy, Daddy's got to help Ms. Vickers install a security system, then we'll go to the zoo."

"Yay!" She clapped her little hands together and he couldn't help but smile. What a bright and happy soul.

"Here you go, Emersyn. I have coloring books, crayons, markers that smell great and some blank paper in case you prefer to draw your own picture. Can I get you some apple juice?"

"Yay! Yes, I want juice."

"Emmy, say please." Dane reminded her.

"Please."

Keirnan smiled and went to the refrigerator while he sat on the sofa unpacking the security system from the package. Reading over the directions to remind himself of the installation steps, he half listened to Keirnan pulling juice from the refrigerator and a cup from the cupboard as Emmy sat at the kitchen table chatting away with her.

A glint of sunlight streamed through the window and he glanced up to see the white Lincoln slowing down in front of the house. Jumping up from the sofa, he practically ran to the door to see if he could get a better look at the driver. All he could see was someone with longer hair as they passed the house. Sandy brownish in color. Nothing else, but it was definitely the same car.

Turning from the door he saw Keirnan standing between the kitchen and living room, a look of fear on her face.

"Was that him?" She whispered.

"Or her. All I saw was longer hair."

She swallowed what appeared to be a large lump in her throat, and he said, "It'll be okay, Keirnan." Then he proceeded to install the security system.

An hour and a half later, he picked up the instructions, discarded the packaging and wire ties that held the wires in place in the package. Walking to the kitchen he tossed them in the waste basket and smiled at Keirnan and Emmy sitting at the kitchen table coloring together.

"When you're finished coloring your picture, I want to show you how this system works. Then, we can go to the zoo."

Emmy dropped her pink crayon, jumped from her chair and clapped her hands together. "I'm ready."

"It'll just be a little bit, Emmy. Finish your picture while I show Keirnan how to use this system."

The smile left her adorable little face, but she solemnly climbed back on her chair and picked up her pink crayon and began coloring a deer's face with it.

He waited for Keirnan to proceed him, then followed behind, glancing briefly at her fine denim encased backside.

"To set your system you punch in this code, 9378-set. When you enter the house, you will have 60 seconds to disarm the system, by entering your code and pushing, Disarm."

"Got it. 9378 - set and 9378 - disarm."

"You're a quick study."

She smiled her brilliant smile. "Thank you. I've always been a fairly quick study. It comes in handy."

"I bet it does."

"Here are your cameras." He pointed to a camera in the corner of the living room, one in the kitchen and one in the hallway just outside of her bedroom door. Walking into her bedroom, he stood by the window, "All of your windows are set with a sensor." Lifting the window her alarm beeped continuously. Closing the window he clicked a remote in his hand. "This is for you to keep by the bed. I've programmed the alarm to be managed with your phone, too. There are also sensors on the garage windows and doors."

Pulling up the app on her phone, he showed her the icon then handed her the phone. Opening the window once more he nodded to her to and watched with pride as she disarmed the alarm using her phone.

"You're a natural, Keirnan. I've also got the app on my phone so I can help you monitor it."

She giggled and the pink that tinted her cheeks was adorable. Unable to resist, he walked to her and pulled her into his arms. His heartbeat sped up when her arms instantly wrapped around his waist. Kissing her softly he enjoyed the feel of her soft damp lips as they accepted his kiss and molded to his as if they were meant to be.

Giggling from his right, had them pulling apart, but only slightly, as he looked down to see Emersyn giggling at them.

"I saw you kiss Ms. Vickers."

"Yes, you did. Does that bother you?"

He glanced at Keirnan who pulled away from him and faced Emmy. Her cheeks were a sexy shade of pink, her lips plumped from his kiss and the way she looked at his daughter made his heart melt. She knelt down in front of Emersyn holding her hands.

"I really like you so much Emersyn, I think you know that. I also really like your dad, too. When grown-ups like each other, sometimes they kiss."

"I know."

"How do you know?"

"I saw Gram kiss Mr. Thomson."

"What?" His voice was louder than he meant it to be. His mom never said anything about a Mr. Thomson, or any man for that matter.

"It was just a pick she said."

Keirnan giggled. "Do you mean a peck?"

"Mmm hmm." Her sweet little head bobbed up and down. Her dark ponytail swished with the movement.

"When did Gram peck Mr. Thomson?"

"Last night when he came over for pie."

Well, this was interesting, and he had to admit, he didn't know how he felt about it at all. Of course, she had a right to be happy and he wanted her to be happy, but he needed to vet Mr. Thomson. That would be the first thing on his list tomorrow.

"Can we go to the zoo now?" Emmy asked Keirnan.

Keirnan's bright smile had Emmy smiling right back. "I think it's time. Can you please go potty first?"

Emmy ran off to the bathroom and Keirnan stood, swiping her hands on her thighs, "I'm embarrassed. We should have spoken to her first before she saw us."

Stepping into her space, he tilted her chin up so her eyes met his. "We should have, but we didn't and we're not going to beat ourselves up over it. She took it well and I enjoy kissing you. She'll be seeing it a lot if I have anything to say about it."

## 17

"So, you'll bring Emmy to *Read with Your Littles* tomorrow night?"

She walked into her kitchen from the living room and set her coffee cup into the sink. Her phone held to her ear with her left hand, she walked down the hall to her bedroom to pull her clothes from her closet for the day.

"We wouldn't miss it. I told Zane that on Thursdays I have to be off no later than four to get home, eat and go with Emmy downtown."

"I'm silly excited about this, Dane. Thank you for bringing her. And, on Saturday, will you still be able to help me set up for the fundraiser? I know I've asked a couple of times, but I'm just reassuring myself."

His laugh on the other end of the phone was deep, throaty and so damned sexy.

"Yes, I'll help you do whatever you need."

"Thank you."

"No need to thank me. Now, how about a dinner date tonight, just you and me? Mom's keeping Emmy."

"Really? That sounds wonderful."

"Okay, so, your place or mine?"

Her nipples pebbled and the shockwaves ran the gamut through her body and centered between her legs. She'd been thinking about making love to him for a few days now. They'd been seeing each other a couple of weeks, close to it, but dang, she was so darned ready. If he were here now she'd even consider calling in a substitute for today.

"Mine. I'll make baked chicken and veggies."

"I didn't mean you needed to cook; I just want to spend time alone with you."

Heat crawled up her body lighting every sense on fire.

"I want to cook for you, and I want to spend time alone with you, too."

His voice took on a growly quality and dang if that wasn't sexy.

"I'll bring wine and dessert. How about six?"

Her voice came out barely more than a whisper.

"Perfect."

"Later, Princess."

"Bye." It was all she could manage before the line went dead.

She allowed herself a moment to sigh. Then, she began pulling clothes from her closet. Dark blue dress slacks, and a white sweater with intricate beading at the V-neck. It had been a gift from her mom when she got this teaching job. Next, she grabbed her under garments and headed to the bathroom to start the water warming for her shower. She'd see Dane briefly this morning when he dropped Emmy off at school, but she wouldn't get to kiss him there. That would have to wait until tonight. She was so danged excited the day would crawl by for sure.

Turning the water on in the shower, she undressed from the sweatpants and tank top she'd slept in and folded them up neatly setting them on the toilet lid. Pulling a clean towel and wash cloth from the bathroom cabinet she tossed them over the shower rod, then locked the bathroom door and climbed into the shower allowing the warm water to slide over her body. The naughty thoughts that ran through her mind excited her, causing her nerves to sizzle, which was a stark contrast to the warm soothing water. Tonight was the night and she couldn't wait.

As she rinsed her hair loud beeping penetrated her mind as she tried to place the sound. Definitely not police or ambulance. It finally dawned on her that it was her new security system.

Shutting off the water and jumping from the shower, she toweled off briefly and tossed her sweatpants and tank back on, feeling less exposed. Listening at the door for sounds of anyone in her house, she tried to get her heart to stop pounding so she could think. Glancing around she realized her phone wasn't in here; she'd left it on the foot of her bed when selecting her clothes for the day.

Her hands shook but she really had no choice but to open the door and run to her bedroom for her phone. Closing her eyes she took two deep breaths, she let the last one out slowly, and softly unlocked the bathroom door. Pulling it back only slightly, the beeping grew louder. She couldn't see anyone in the hallway. Looking across the hall to her bedroom, she didn't see signs of anyone in there, either. She opened the door and ran across the hall to her bedroom and slammed the door closed, turning the lock in place. Swiftly picking up her phone she first ran to her closet and looked inside. No one inside meant she was moderately safe in here. Debating between jumping from the window or waiting until police arrived, she remembered Dane telling her to run from danger if she had the chance. If not, she should hide. Trouble was, there weren't many places in here to hide that weren't obvious to someone looking.

Angry with herself for feeling so scatterbrained right now, she shook her head again quickly trying to clear it, then froze when the alarm suddenly went silent. Her heartbeat sped up at a rapid pace, and fear caused her to grow warm and perspire. Unsure what else to do, she closed the closet door and hid behind the long dresses she had at the back. Former prom dresses, a bridesmaid's dress from her friend Gail's wedding and the dress she intended to wear this Saturday to the fundraiser. Standing as close to the back wall as possible, she tried evening her breathing so she wouldn't be heard. Swallowing the acid that gathered in her mouth she willed herself to not throw up.

Suddenly she heard someone trying to open her bedroom door. Twisting the knob back and forth then adding a bit of force before she heard the loud thud as a body slammed into the door. Covering her mouth with her right hand she stifled a scream and tried calculating how long she still had and whether she could make it to the window in time.

Deciding to take the chance she scrambled from the closet, another loud thud sounded against the door and the wood began to crack. Then another before she heard the male voice, "Open the door."

## 18

-----

"Keirnan, open the door, it's me, Dane."

He tried the knob once again, then tried bursting through one more time. His heart raced and his mind couldn't get past the fact that she might be in there and in danger.

"Keirnan, open the door if you can."

"Dane?"

Her voice was strained but it sounded so damned good. "Yes, are you okay? Can you open the door?"

After what seemed like minutes, he heard the lock click on the other side of the door handle and the door opened.

The instant she came into view she threw herself into his body and he was so off guard, he only had a split second to brace himself before wrapping his arms completely around her body.

She felt good. Fantastic against him, but his brain struggled with the feeling that someone had set off the alarm and he needed to set the feel of her body aside and investigate the area.

"Are you hurt?" he managed.

"No. Just scared."

She released her grip on him and slid down his body. The first thing he noticed was the skimpy wet tank top she wore and perfectly shaped nipples straining to be free. The darkness of her nipples visible through the wet fabric and his cock pulsed and thickened.

"Jesus." He muttered. "Okay, I need to go see what caused the alarm to go off and you need..." He glanced at her body again noticing more dampness from her long, wet hair at various places along her torso. Fucking sexy. "...to get some clothes on."

Before he lost his resolve, he turned and left her room, stepped into the spare bedroom, checked the closet. All clear.

Moving down the hallway to the living room and kitchen areas he checked each place a person could hide, the linen closet, entry closet, and pantry, though small, a determined person could hide in there. Then he went through the mud room to the backdoor and dread landed like a hot rock in his stomach. Someone had used a crowbar or something similar to pry the backdoor open. Likely the alarm scared them away, but still someone was getting closer.

"Did you find what caused the alarm to go off?"

Turning to see Keirnan, now sadly encased in a gray, terry cloth robe, he captured her eyes with his and nodded.

"It looks like someone was trying to break in through the backdoor."

Her right hand flew to cover her mouth, her eyes rounded, fear evident in them. "Oh my God!" she exclaimed.

"It doesn't appear they were successful, the alarm likely scared them away."

Lowering her hand she tucked silky strands of damp hair behind her ear.

"Now I'm starting to get this eerie sensation on my skin. This is all so weird, and I don't understand it at all."

"Has anyone given you reason to feel like you are in danger? Anyone said anything, or acted strange at all besides the man in the library?"

He watched her as she obviously tried to determine her level of danger. Her bright shiny eyes were now clouded with fear; but the dark green color was so beautiful with her coloring.

"I can't think of anyone else."

He checked the lock on the door, felt confident that it was still secure, though the metal on the storm door was scratched and dented. Then he stepped closer to her and wrapped her in his arms. All these protective, soft feelings washed over him and he wrestled with pushing them away. He hadn't loved anyone since Catherine, and he could feel his heart reaching for Keirnan. It scared him just as much as it excited him.

"It'll be okay. I'll do everything I can to protect you. I'm confident Auggie will as well."

Her arms wrapped around his waist and pulled him tight to her body and his heart felt full. He rested his cheek against her hair and inhaled her scent. She squeezed him once then released him and stepped back.

"How did you get here so fast?"

He chuckled. "I just dropped Emmy off at mom's before school because I was going over to Astec early this morning when I got an alert on my phone that your alarm tripped. I sped over here and found the door locked. I had to force my way in when you didn't answer the door. I'll fix that."

Her eyes sought his and her full lips curved into that smile he enjoyed so much. "I'm glad you were so close."

He smiled at her in return. "Me, too."

Her cheeks tinted pink before she spoke, utterly adorable. "I hate to ask, but now I'm a bit weirded out and I haven't finished my shower. Do you mind staying while I shower and get ready for work?"

That was going to be hard. Thinking of her in the shower, naked, wet and sexy while he sat out here waiting was going to be hard, but he'd do it.

"Of course, it will give me time to fix your doors and make sure the locks are situated."

"Thank you."

She turned and headed out of the mud room and through the kitchen and he waited a beat to get his body under control before turning to do as he promised, fix her locks and the front and backdoors.

He stepped out to his truck briefly to grab his toolbox from the back, and headed back into the house before she got out of the shower. Starting with the front door, which surprisingly didn't have the best lock in town as it was, he unscrewed the knob from the door. He made quick work of adding a new steel plate behind it, and reattached the lock, making sure the alarm system was still in place and working. Then he tackled the back door and lock.

Keirnan emerged from the back of the house about a half hour later, looking like the Princess he thought she was. Dark blue slacks, a white beaded sweater and her hair pulled back into a messy bun at the back of her head. Her lips were tinted a light pink and shined where light from the window touched them and her lashes were darkened just a bit. She was stunning.

"You look gorgeous, Keirnan."

Her cheeks brightened again but she graced him with that smile he was falling so hard for and replied, "Thank you. I feel beautiful every time you tell me that."

Setting his tools in the box, he walked to her and kissed her lips, softly, only wanting the slightest of tastes before pulling back.

"I'll tell you every day if you like because it's true."

She giggled and that sound made his heart grow another size larger.

"Now, tell me this. Are you sure you feel comfortable coming back here alone after work or would you like to go to my house? I have an extra key."

He pulled it from his pocket, intending to give it to her tonight because it just felt right.

"Are you sure?"

"I wouldn't offer it if I weren't. I'll text you the entry code to the house."

She swallowed then looked into his eyes as she took his key. "Thank you, I really don't feel that comfortable in my own house right now."

" Grab some clothes, and go straight to my house today after school. If you want to cook, great, if not, we'll order to go and eat at home. I'll ask mom to keep Emmy."

## 19

S he sat in her car staring at Dane's house, her stomach alight with butterflies. This was surreal and the fact that he trusted her to go into his house alone, well that just blew her away. Though she trusted him in her house. She had nothing to hide, so there was that. And that's what made this so special, clearly he had nothing to hide, either.

Taking in a deep breath she reached for her purse from the passenger seat, opened her car door and got out. Opening the backdoor she pulled her overnight bag from the backseat and turned to walk into Dane's home.

The outside was brick, a darker brown brick and the trim around the windows and doors was a soft creamy tan. It was striking and calming at the same time. While most people had a bright colored front door, Dane decided to forego that, and it worked. Or maybe it was Catherine who'd wanted it that way.

The mere thought of Catherine sent a jolt of dread through her body. He must have loved her very much. She'd died so young and with an infant at home, too. He hadn't moved on in five years and that said something right there. It was hard to compete with a dead woman, not that she was competing, but a person had a way of remembering only the good once a person was gone. That meant the things about her that might bug the heck out of him would stand out glaringly.

Reaching the front door, she inserted the gold key he'd given her this morning and took the deepest breath her lungs could hold. Letting it out slowly, she twisted the knob and opened the door. Stepping into the entry way, she turned to the left where Dane said she'd find the alarm keypad, and entered the code. Inhaling, she waited for the beep to confirm she'd entered correctly. Relief swam through her when the beep sounded and she closed the front door and twisted the lock in place. Turning to the living room she found beautiful dark hardwood floors and a large rug in the center of the room, a plush tan with burgundy, black and dark brown circles on it, which added a touch of fun. The brown leather sofa was comfy looking and inviting. Burgundy throw pillows were strewn about the sofa and a burgundy blanket was folded and laid across the back of it. A matching loveseat sat to the right of the sofa with matching pillows.

She set her overnight bag on the floor next to the sofa and slipped her shoes off and set them alongside her bag. Opening her purse she deposited her keys inside, zipped it closed and laid it on her shoes.

Walking through the living room to the kitchen in the rear, she smiled at the neatness of the room, its soft creamy walls and glistening granite countertops in deep brown with coppery flecks. Stainless appliances shined and her heart fluttered just a bit. It was beautiful. Turning to the refrigerator, she admired three drawings Emmy had made and colored. One of them tugged at her heart a bit as it was a drawing of a little girl and a much larger figure. Above the tall figure she wrote 'Daddy' and above the smaller figure she wrote 'me'. Sweet and yet sad at the same time. Deciding to see what she could make for supper she began pulling out the makings for a salad. Opening the freezer, she found a frozen chicken and wondered if she'd have enough time to make it before Dane came home.

There was a pantry door to the left of the refrigerator, and she opened it to find an InstaPot on the bottom shelf. Perfect.

Taking it from the pantry she set it on the counter and pulled up her phone to search for a recipe. Excitement began running through her at the thought of making Dane a dinner in his own home and spending the night here with him.

The table was set and the kitchen smelled heavenly. Nothing left to do now but wait for the timer to sound and Dane to get home. Deciding to investigate a bit more she walked back into the living room and took a closer look. The fireplace directly across from the sofa was made of the same color brick as the outside and the dark wooden mantle was the same color as the floor. Very striking and yet not at all pretentious. Picture frames lined the mantle and she walked to take a closer look.

Dane and Emersyn in recent days, it looked like at the zoo, both smiling and happy probably this summer gauging by Emersyn's age in the photo. The next was Dane, Emmy and his mom, Estella. A picture in the middle was a beautiful blond woman holding a very tiny baby. Her smile was breathtaking and the joy in her face was clear to see. Catherine and Emersyn she'd suppose. There was another picture of Catherine wearing a pair of jeans and a pretty red t-shirt, no shoes, her hair in pig tails and that same mesmerizing smile. She leaned against a tree; her arms crossed.

"That was the week before she died."

Squealing she whipped around to see Dane standing in the doorway to the living room from the kitchen.

He chuckled, "I didn't mean to startle you."

"I'm sorry to yelp, I was just engrossed in your pictures." She glanced at the picture of Catherine once again, and softly said, "She was beautiful." She looked at him once again.

His smile seemed reverent, maybe a bit sad. "She was as beautiful inside as she was outside."

"So is Emmy."

His smile turned into a big grin. "She certainly is." He came to her and kissed her lips softly. "I see you decided to make dinner. What are we having?"

The timer went off and she giggled. "Chicken, wild rice and salad."

"Sounds fantastic. Do I have time to jump in the shower? I got a bit grungy today."

"Sure, I have to pull the chicken from the pot and toss the salad."

He kissed her briefly again, turned and headed down the hall. She was eager to see the rest of the house, but she wanted him to show her.

Heading to the kitchen she began releasing the steam from the pressure cooker as she pulled the salad from the refrigerator.

Setting out the dressing he had in the refrigerator she then turned to pull the chicken and rice from the pot. Locating two large serving forks she stabbed the chicken, lifted it out and laid it on a plate. Spooning the rice from the pan she surrounded the chicken with the rice and smiled at the picture it made.

"It smells fantastic in here." His deep voice floated over her and excitement coursed through her. It felt like the beginning right now. Right here. At this moment, they were starting their relationship in earnest.

## 20

"Supper was delicious." He watched her cheeks deepen in color and she looked stunning.

"Thank you."

He stood, laid his fork and knife across his plate and carried them all to the counter. Returning, he did the same with Keirnan's. She stood and began to help clear the table and he let his thoughts wonder if it could be this way always. The realization that he'd been lonely these past few years settled in his stomach like a punch. He thought he kept himself busy enough to not feel that loneliness set in, but it did anyway.

"Do you rinse before putting them in the dishwasher?"

"No, no need."

Carrying the leftover food to the counter, he began putting it into glass container and sealing it with a lid, then putting it in the refrigerator. Turning to see her wiping the counter off, she rinsed the dish cloth in the sink, then laid it across the divider between the two sinks.

When she turned to face him, he didn't hesitate a beat. Walking the few steps to her he wrapped her in his arms and kissed her. Like he wanted to kiss her when he came home. His tongue slipped between her lips and he heard her sigh. Her arms encircled his neck as her lips and tongue danced with his. She tasted like the finest meal he'd ever had, and she felt much, much better.

His heart danced in time with their tongues, each slide and dip of his was matched by Keirnan. Her breathing increased and he could feel her heartbeat increase against his chest. His hands moved down her back and cupped her delicious ass and she moaned. He pulled her in close so her body rocked against his hardened cock and the friction felt fantastic.

He pulled away only enough to whisper, "I want you, Keirnan."

When she responded, "I want you, too," he wasted no time. Bending to pick her up, he cradled her in his arms, hers still wrapped around his neck. She looked up at him, her kiss swollen lips a deep pink from the pressure of his lips, but they split open to a gorgeous smile and he felt his heart expand again.

"You're simply beautiful."

Her head cocked to the side as she examined his face, his eyes, his hair, he half watched her perusal as he carried her down the hall to his bedroom. As they entered the room, rather than put her down he looked into her dark green eyes.

"You are simply the handsomest man I've ever met in my life, Dane Copeland, and I'm not just saying that to get into your pants."

Then she giggled and he burst out laughing. Kissing her lips once more, he said, "Well, just so you know, even if you were, it worked."

He set her on the bed and she scooted up to the

pillows. He followed her, eager to taste her lips again, eager to touch her. Eager for everything.

Laying over her body, his cock hardened further when her legs spread open to make room for him between them. Her hair laid across the pillow and looked like the softest satin. He kissed his way down her neck, inhaling the fragrance of her perfume, the lingering shower soap he smelled on her this morning and his body responded more.

Kissing down her chest to the neck of her sweater, he'd had enough of their clothing. Rearing back on his knees, he pulled his shirt from his pants, and was pleased to see Keirnan pull her sweater over her head. The blush colored bra she wore was beautifully delicate in color and material. Soft lace cupped her breasts perfectly and he couldn't stop his hands from reaching out and running his fingers along the edge where her bra ended and her skin began.

Goosebumps rose on her skin and he smiled. Then he saw the front clasp on her bra and smiled as his fingers pinched the fabric on either side and released her fantastic breasts from their confines. Her nipples puck-ered to tight points and his tongue instantly sought to shower them with kisses and nibble on them.

Her moans urged him on and he laved each nipple with enough attention that he thought he'd burst right out of his pants. Kissing his way down to the waistband of her slacks, he stopped, unfastened the button and lowered the zipper.

Peeling the fabric open he saw the matching panties but decided as sexy as she looked in her delicate fabric, he had waited a couple of weeks to get to where they were right now and he was tired of waiting.

As if she knew what he was thinking, she raised her hips and he quickly tugged her slacks and panties down them, then she lifted her legs, bent at the knee to make it easier for him to remove them from her completely. Sexy.

He began removing the rest of his clothing as she gave her bra a tug from under her and dropped it off the edge of the bed with the rest of her clothing.

The second he was naked he crawled up her body, stopping at the light curls between her legs. Unable to resist tasting her, his tongue sought her center, and her response was enough to let him know she was thinking the same thing he was. She sighed loudly as his tongue slid up and down between her lips. Her scent drove him on, she tasted as sweet as she smelled and it all called to him. Her soft skin massaging his cheeks, her soft moans of pleasure, her fingers combing through his hair, the pulsing of her hips. She was hypnotic.

Sucking her clit into his mouth and flicking it with his tongue, she arched her back and gasped in pleasure. He repeated his attentions on her until he heard her gasp his name and she fisted her fingers in his hair. That. Was. Fucking. Sexy.

Her taste exploded on his tongue and he eagerly lapped up every drop before continuing to crawl up her body.

His lips planted on hers, he kissed her, thrusting his tongue into her mouth so she could taste just how delicious she was. Arching his back, he positioned his throbbing cock at the opening of her body and wanted to thrust inside of her, but she stiffened.

Backing away just slightly he kissed her cheek, reached over to the nightstand and opened the top drawer. Grabbing the new condom box from inside he made haste ripping the top off and pulling out a condom. Using his teeth, he tore the top off the foil packet as he tossed the box back into the drawer.

Rolling the condom onto his painfully hard cock, he pumped himself a couple of times and Keirnan lifted her head to watch him.

"That's so sexy, she whispered, then licked her lips.

"Not as sexy as you coming on my tongue."

"Hmm, I don't know about that, but watching you right now, that's just amazing."

Her voice was almost a whisper, then her eyes looked into his.

"I'll show you amazing, Keirnan. Watch me as I disappear inside of you."

He positioned his cock at her entrance as she lifted herself up on her elbows. Both of them watched as he slowly pushed himself inside of her, pulled out slightly and slid back in.

"Ooh my God." She whispered then fell back to the pillow and lifted her legs to wrap them around his ass. From that position, he was able to fully seat himself inside of her and the feeling was extraordinary. He closed his eyes to get himself under control, the feel of her warm wetness cupping him tightly as he slid in and out was like heaven.

When her legs tightened to push him in further, well, that was fucking sexy.

He glanced down at her body as he pumped in and out of her, her full breasts swayed, her puckered nipples strained toward him, her face showed all signs of pleasure and he wanted to watch her as she came again, he missed it last time.

Pushing into her he ground himself tight against her

and she gasped at the feel. That was the spot right there. Hitting it again and again he continued to push in, grind against her, pull out and do it again.

Her breathing quickened, her fingers dug into his ass, her feet pushed him harder and his pace quickened. He just hoped he could get her there before he blew, because he was fucking close right now.

"Dane," she gasped.

"Dane." Her hips lifted and he ground against her hard. "Oh...fuck..."

Her lips formed an "O", in ecstasy as she reached her orgasm which created the most compelling look on her face and he wanted to see that again and again, but right now, he had his own completion in mind. He pumped again and again as his balls drew up painfully tight and he exploded. White stars floated in his vision, his breathing was ragged as if he'd just run a marathon and his heart hammered in his chest.

He strained not to fall on top of her, but her arms pulled him down and wrapped tightly around him, so he let go. Her legs tightened against him, her uneven breathing against his ear matched his own.

## 21

Opening her eyes she looked at the wall she was facing. Dane's arms were wrapped around her, his front to her back, his breathing deep and steady. She'd dozed for a while, that was the first time she'd done that. In the past, she'd had boyfriends, only two she'd slept with, one her senior year of high school and if they had sex, it was in a car. Her college boyfriend always jumped up and ran out of her room almost immediately after they were finished having sex. It only took her a month to realize he just wanted to get laid and, frankly, she wanted to focus on her studies anyway, so she told him to take a hike. She felt foolish now, because in that respect, Dane was much more experienced than she was.

He inhaled deeply, then softly said, "What are you thinking about?"

Turning her head to see his face she smiled as his tousled hair looked sexy. Mostly because she was the one who'd tousled it.

"What makes you think I'm thinking about something?"

"You stiffened up, relaxed, stiffened up again. Thinking."

Rolling over onto her back she stared at the ceiling. Not wanting to completely spoil the mood, but also wanting to make sure this relationship was open in all things she took a breath.

"I would like to ask you a couple of questions. If you don't mind."

He chuckled, raised himself up so his head rested in his hand and looked down at her.

"Okay, I'm ready."

She turned and mimicked his position facing him. "You kissed me in front of Catherine's picture. Do you do...have you done that before. Kissed a woman in front of her picture?"

He wrinkled his nose a moment, then touched her cheek with his left forefinger, smoothing a few strands of hair from her cheek.

"No. I've never had another woman here before. Unless you count my mom."

She winced slightly, then laughed. "No, I don't count her." Rethinking her words she shook her head, "I mean, she counts, but not like that."

His smile was beguiling. His chuckle came from deep in his chest.

Swallowing she ventured further. "I mean...was that hard?"

"Yes."

"But you did it anyway?"

"Obviously."

"But, I don't understand. I mean, why?"

She looked deep into his eyes and she saw a flash of pain, then of letting go. "Keirnan, when Catherine died I thought I would go mad. I loved her and Emmy so much. They were my life. My whole life. I wanted a dozen kids with her. I looked forward to coming home from missions." Taking a deep breath, she watched as he continued to explain and she swallowed the little green monster that tried to crawl from her stomach.

"The day she died a piece of me died. I didn't sleep. I didn't eat. I had a hard time coping. The bastard that was drunk and killed her got only eighteen months in jail. He killed a beautiful, vibrant, loving wife and mother and he only got eighteen months in jail. I wanted to kill him. I wanted his family to feel what I felt. I plotted. I waited. I worked. It's how I got through the days that followed. By the time he got out of jail, in eleven months because the fucker got out on good behavior, if you can believe that bullshit, I was ready. I snuck into his house in the middle of the night. I was going to walk in, shoot him and walk out. My anger was so strong nothing else mattered. Nothing. I stood by his bedside and watched him sleep, his wife on the other side and I felt enraged that he was able to lay next to his wife while mine was dead and in the ground."

"Oh my God, Dane." She whispered it.

"He opened his eyes and looked at me. The moon was bright enough that he could see me. He looked at me for a few minutes, then he nodded at me and closed his eyes. Like he was giving me permission. It was then that I realized that he had to live with the knowledge that he killed someone. He must have hated himself as much as I hated him. I turned and left." He cleared his throat and inhaled deeply as if to cleanse his lungs. "I told my mom what I did. She asked me to get help, so I did. And one of the things that my counselor told me was that I had to move on. Life isn't fair. For anyone. I'm no different. I have to make my life worth something and I have to make sure Emmy has at least one parent to raise her."

"I'm glad you want that for her." She reached forward and took his hand in hers and squeezed.

"When I came home tonight and I saw you looking at her picture I knew that was a moment that would mean something to both of us. Apparently I was right, you noticed it, too. She'll always be part of me, Keirnan, but she isn't between us. Does that make sense?"

"Yes, it does. And, for the record, I'm not threatened in the sense that I think she is between us, only that you'll likely only remember the good parts of life with her, and with me, however long we're together, you'll likely see the not-so-nice stuff. It's part of the package though, I'm afraid."

His chuckle was genuine and her heart beat wildly that he saw the humor she wanted to convey on this hugely serious topic.

"I'm afraid you'll see some not-so-nice stuff with me, too, Princess." He turned and stood from the bed, pulling on his underwear he smiled so beautifully and said, "Now, how about some dessert?"

## 22

"Okay Emmy, come on, we have to go or we'll be late."

"Ms. Vickers said I could bring a stuffed animal to cuddle with while we read and I can't find Teddy." She whined.

"Did you take Teddy to Gram's last night?"

She froze, her little face in the beginning stages of a meltdown. "Tell you what, let's get on our way to the library and I'll call Gram while we're in the car and see if she can bring Teddy to the library."

"Yay." Emmy jumped up and down and clapped her hands and he was relieved he didn't have to navigate another five-year-old outburst. They'd been happening here and there lately; his mom said she thought it was because so much was going on with his job and Keirnan and Emmy may be feeling like Keirnan will replace her. That's why tonight was so important.

"Okay, come on then, let's get into the truck."

He took her hand and led her through the kitchen and

to the garage. Lifting her up into the backseat he waited as she climbed into her car seat, then proceeded to buckle her in.

Climbing into the driver's seat he buckled up, tapped the garage door button and started the truck. Once he had backed out, he closed the garage door, then tapped the call icon on his dash to call his mom.

She answered on the second ring. "I thought you were on your way to the reading program."

"We are. Emmy left Teddy at your house. Is there a possibility you might be going out tonight and can bring him to the library?"

"As a matter of fact, we're getting ready to go out to dinner, we'll swing by. Then you can meet Stan."

"Stan?" Must be that Mr. Thomson Emmy saw her "peck".

"Yes, Dane, Stan. We've been seeing each other recently. He's very nice."

His eyes darted to Emmy by way of the rearview mirror then back to the road. "I'm sure he is Mom."

"We'll be there in a few minutes. Stan is just pulling into the drive now."

"Okay, see you in a bit."

His stomach twisted a little. He figured this would happen eventually. His mom was attractive, vibrant and amazing. But, now that she was seeing someone, he wasn't sure he liked it much. Shaking his head to clear his mind, he silently decided not to pass judgment until he got a bit more information on Stan. Realization that in some ways this must be how Emmy was feeling, had him reflecting on how to make Emmy feel more comfortable about Keirnan being in their lives. He also needed for Emmy to know that he still wanted those special times only with her.

Turning into the library parking lot, there were very few spaces left to park. Keirnan was likely worried that they wouldn't show. Finding a place at the far end of the lot, he jumped from the truck, opened the backdoor and began unbuckling Emmy from her car seat.

Lifting her out, he set her down and tapped his key fob as they began walking to the door of the library. Another car pulled in as they were walking up the steps, so at least they weren't the last to arrive.

Pulling open the large, ornate wooden door he ushered Emmy through before following her in. Taking her hand once again he chuckled when she began pulling him to the reading room. She loved this story time.

"Daddy, there's Ms. Vickers," Emmy exclaimed as she dropped his hand and ran toward Keirnan.

As usual Keirnan was stunning. Everything about her called to him. The smile she bestowed on Emmy was amazing. The smile on Emmy's face was just as amazing. Keirnan knelt down so she was eye to eye with Emmy and as he approached he heard Emmy prattling off her story about Teddy.

Keirnan listened to every word, then said, "I'll help you keep an eye out for Gram."

Then she stood and shined her smile on him, and he felt like it was a spotlight it was so bright.

"Hi, glad you were able to make it."

"I'm sorry we're almost late, as you heard, we couldn't find Teddy."

She giggled and nodded.

"I like your necklace, Ms. Vickers."

Keirnan reached for her necklace and lovingly touched the glinting purple stone at the end. "Thank you. I got this necklace from my grandmother on my sixteenth birthday. It's an amethyst, my birthstone."

Emmy tried unsuccessfully a couple of times to say Amethyst and then gave up.

"Here you go, dear." His mom said from behind them and Emmy excitedly took Teddy from her hands as Dane turned to meet Stan.

Introductions were made, then Keirnan saved him from any awkwardness when she said, "You are welcome to stay for story time, but I do have to get things underway."

"Go dear and start things, the kids will get restless and we have reservations to meet."

He shook Stan's hand and was mildly impressed with the firm handshake he returned. Okay, so that was a point in his favor.

"Dane, just find a book or two that you and Emmy want to read, then find a beanbag chair or pillow and sit where you like."

He wanted to kiss her, but he settled for a wink, which earned him a big smile and a blush. Almost as good. He and Emmy found a couple of books and a beanbag chair, something he hadn't sat in for years, and they flopped against the far wall so he could watch everything going on. Old habits die hard.

Keirnan clapped her hands, "Thank you all so much for coming out tonight. I'll be around as usual if you have questions or need me to watch your little ones while you use the restroom. And as a reminder, this Saturday is the fundraiser for the library, so if you can give even just a little, it will all be so helpful. We're specifically focusing on the windows, updating the elevator, flooring and the roof which needs to be repaired. Next year, if all goes well, we'll focus on furniture and new books. Thank you."

She earned a round of applause, which had her blushing crimson but her smile stole the show. Then she stepped back and walked to the front desk and the low murmuring of parents reading to their children filled the room. He read to Emmy, though he kept his eye on Keirnan. He watched as she picked up a box and walked to the back area of the library, where she mentioned that she stored the decorations for the fundraiser. She was always working.

Finishing the first book Emmy had picked out, he looked around and didn't see Keirnan. A quick glance around the room showed him that no one else seemed concerned so he began reading the second book.

Turning the fourth page of the book, he glanced around again and now his gut tightened. She still hadn't come back to the room. Another mom also seemed to be looking for her. Looking at the front desk, he saw a woman sitting at the computer, so he told Emmy to stay put and he'd be right back. Leaning over to the mom and daughter next to them, he asked, "Excuse me, would you mind watching Emmy for just a moment?"

"Not at all. Usually Keirnan is around but I don't see her."

He nodded and stood. "I'll be right back, Emmy."

Walking to the front desk, he said, "Excuse me, would you mind watching my daughter while I go back and make sure Keirnan is alright? She's been gone quite a while."

The woman looked to the hallway Keirnan had disappeared down, then stood and walked to the counter. Holding her hand out, she said, "Hi I'm Bekah Dodson, the library curator."

## 23

Setting the awkward, but not heavy, box on one of the well-worn library tables in the back room, Keirnan pushed it all the way to the wall and dusted her hands on her thighs. Turning to exit the room, she noticed two tables stacked on top of each other, which hadn't been like that before. She recalled Bekah's comments about some furniture being moved around, and she wondered if this was what she meant. She'd have to ask her.

Stepping out of the room she heard a faint distressed voice crying, "Help me, please."

"Hello?" She walked in the direction of the voice and heard the distressed cry once again. "Please, help me."

The second room was dark, and the voice sounded further away than that; so, she walked to the last room on this side of the library, where she'd seen the long-haired man a couple of weeks ago. Bracing herself in case he was still sitting there, she called out once again. "Hello, can I help you?"

"Oh yes, please." The voice responded. Walking to the

far-right corner of the room she pushed open a door, which she thought was a closet.

Immediately her mouth was covered with a rough hand and her body was pulled against a hard chest with an iron band of an arm secured around her waist. Stunned she froze for a split second, then began kicking back at her attacker. She caught his shin at one point and heard him hiss out his displeasure at her as soon as she connected. She tried twisting her body to break his grasp but that earned her a tightened grip and tersely threatening words whispered in her ear. "Keep it up ya little bitch and you'll die right here."

Her first thought was the horror the kids in the library would feel at finding her dead. Her next thought was that she didn't want to die.

Opening her mouth as much as she could to bite the fingers across her face had him dropping his hold for a split second, then harshly pulling her back. His right arm, previously wrapped around her waist, came up and slapped her on the side of the head, then his fingers closed around her neck. "Keep it up and you die now."

Spots swam before her eyes as she tried to breathe, a tug on her necklace reminded her it was there, but though she fought it, she lost consciousness.

The cold crisp air woke her, and she realized she was bound with duct tape at her wrists and ankles. Chilled, her body shaking, which could also be from fright, had her trying desperately to figure out where she was. This place, wherever it was, didn't smell like the library, it smelled like blood or death or other scary things. Her heartbeat increased, her ears throbbed, and the scent of musty air similar to an old heating vent or damp basement penetrated her nostrils. Panic threatened to set in, but she squeezed her eyes closed and focused on her breathing. In then out slowly, repeat. Trying to recall all of the survival training her father had instilled in her, she remembered, she needed to find a straight surface to try and weaken the tape. The dimly lit room didn't offer her a lot of visuals, but luckily she could make out a metal shelving unit across the room. Bracing herself with her hands, her wrists taped in front of her, she slowly righted herself from her tilted position until she sat upright. She stopped to listen for a few seconds and hearing nothing, she began to scoot over to the shelves. The floor was damp and wet, and she tried not to think of the crawly things that likely lived in the room, wherever it was.

Moving as fast as she could across the floor scooting on her butt, she also used her hands and heels to dig into the floor, even though like her wrists her ankles were taped together; she made her way to the shelves. Shivering and lightheaded she wondered if they'd drugged her. She felt like she did when she took cold medicine, nothing quite clear, and yet, not unclear either. Stopping again to listen and make sure no one could hear her, she was met with only silence. One more scoot and she could reach the shelves. Dragging her butt along, all the while trying to loosen the tape around her ankles as she dug in her heels, she stopped when pain shot through her legs. Scooting next to the shelving, she began running the tape around her wrists along the underside of the bottom shelf, which was about a foot off the ground, hoping she could find a sharp area or open edge to, if not cut, then at least severely weaken the tape. After a few strokes, she felt as though she was making no progress. Reaching her arms forward, she ran her fingers along the underside of the shelf looking for a sharp spot or broken area to use.

Finding a spot where the shelf felt as though it had buckled and there was a sharp crack in the bracing she almost gasped at her good fortune, such as it was. Back and forth she ran the tape between her wrists along the bottom of the shelf, beginning to feel as though this was only expending energy she couldn't afford to waste. The tape caught on something on the far edge and she scooted closer to the shelf to be able to reach that spot and make this go quicker.

Once, twice, three times and the tape weakened and she snapped her arms into a downward motion, hoping to finish breaking the tape. No such luck. Trying once more, she lifted her arms above her head and dropped them down, pulling her wrists apart at the same time. The tape broke and she stifled a sob, but she wasn't finished yet. Desperately clawing at the tape around her ankles she tried breaking free, but this tape wasn't like the other tape.

Twisting to the shelf she felt around to see if there was something she could use to cut the tape. Touching a nail, she grabbed it between her thumb and forefinger and ran the sharp end of it up and down the middle of the tape around her ankles. Hearing a tear she increased her pace until she caused the tape to break open.

Inhaling at her stroke of luck, she then began looking around the room to see where the door to get in and, more importantly, out of stood. From there, she'd devise a plan, but she'd have to do it quickly because who knew when they'd come back to check on her.

## 24

"Keirnan?" He walked through the doorway and down the hall to the first room. He saw the box she'd been carrying sitting on the table, so he knew she'd been back here. Looking around the room he couldn't see anyone else. He swiped his hand up the wall looking for a light switch and finally found one. The light flickered to life, the old fixture offering as much light as it could, but not nearly enough for the size of this room.

Turning to leave the room he clicked the light off and pulled his phone from his pocket. Turning the flashlight on, he shone the light on the walls of the hallway, looking for a switch, finding one at the opposite end of the hall. Walking to the end, he glanced into the second room, found the switch and turned it on, only to find it lacking as well. This place really did need a lot of work. Nothing of note here, so he continued on.

"Keirnan?" He called again, the sinking feeling in his stomach beginning to give way to panic. Entering the third room he flicked the light on and the first thing he noticed was a door open to the far right of the room, which he immediately walked to. His stomach somersaulted when he saw Keirnan's broken necklace laying on the floor and no Keirnan. She'd been here, but so had someone else; she surely wouldn't just leave everyone wondering where she was. She wouldn't leave her necklace, either. Checking the floor and shining his flashlight on the old scared wood, he saw footprints in the dust, and drag marks in various positions as if someone were half dragged, half carried out of the room. Following the path as far as he could, it stopped at an old elevator that had an out of order sign on it. Pushing the button to call the elevator, he waited as he heard grinding and groaning. The fear continued to grow in his gut, and he struggled with how long to search on his own and when to call authorities. Deciding to try calling Keirnan's phone, he listened for ringing in case she was simply disoriented and sitting somewhere close by. It rang, but he couldn't hear it ringing anywhere close. He decided to call his mom to come and take Emmy home with her, but his phone rang first.

Not recognizing the number, he answered hesitantly. "Copeland."

"Dane, it's Auggie Vickers. Is Keirnan with you?"

"No, she's disappeared and I'm beginning to worry. I'm at the back of the library searching for her and all I've found so far is her necklace lying on the floor."

"I just got an anonymous phone call telling me that I'd pay with my daughter's life for my mistakes."

"Fuck." He looked around, the bile rising to his throat the fear beginning to suffocate him.

"What does that mean?"

"I don't know. I'll be right there. I'll call the police."

The call ended and he tapped his mom's number, trying to keep his panic at bay.

"Dane, honey, how can I help you?"

"Mom, I need you to come to the library and pick up Emmy. We have a serious situation here."

"What? What's going on?"

"Mom, please just come." He didn't want to sound desperate, but the fear was getting palpable.

"Okay, we'll be right there."

Making his way quickly to the *Reading with Your Littles* program, his panic rising tenfold. He didn't want to disappoint Emmy, but he needed to be in the back looking for Keirnan.

He saw the red and blue lights of the police cruisers flashing through the windows and knew help was now here.

Emmy saw him coming toward her and ran to him, grabbing his hand. "Daddy, where's Ms. Vickers?"

"She's in the back, babe."

"Davey's dad is looking for her and so is Zach's mom."

"Yes, honey, it's a very busy time for Ms. Vickers right now, so let's see if we can help out."

Taking her hand he led her to the front desk, Bekah looked up at him, her smile immediately faltered when she looked into his eyes.

Leaning forward, he softly said, "My mom is on her way to pick up Emmy, but I need to go out and talk to the police, can you give her a little job to do to keep her busy behind the desk here with you? I wouldn't ask if it wasn't important."

Bekah whispered back, "Where is Keirnan?"

"I don't know."

"Daddy?"

"Please, Bekah."

"Yes, yes, of course. Emmy, honey, can you help me organize the snacks?"

"Yay." Her little hands clapped together.

"Emmy, you stay with Ms. Dodson and don't go anywhere else, okay?"

"Okay, Daddy."

He nodded to Bekah as he walked Emmy behind the desk, then rushed out front to speak with police.

Finding the officer in charge, he walked up to him. "I'm Dane Copeland, Keirnan Vickers' boyfriend."

"Mr. Copeland, tell me what happened."

Quickly relaying the information to him, the officer then turned to two officers and nodded for them to go inside.

"Once again Mr. Copeland, tell me exactly what time all of this happened, detail by detail."

His frustration began to rise but he knew he had to stay calm or the officers would begin to suspect him of some wrongdoing. And, honestly, all he wanted was to find Keirnan and take her home with him.

"Dane?" He turned to see his mom and Stan walking up to him.

"Officer, this is my mom and her friend, and I asked her to come and take my daughter home with her. Can I please go in with my mom and get Emmy?"

"Mr. Copeland, we'll go in with you, however, no one is going anywhere until we've done a search and questioned everyone who was present."

His heart sank, they were wasting time. They turned and walked into the library, all heads looked their way and the murmuring started to grow louder.

"Oh, good Lord, this is going to be a long night," the officer muttered.

---

## 25

His frustration was at an all-time high. This wasn't what he was used to. He and his men went in and got the job done. This questioning and standing around while Keirnan was nowhere to be found, and no one was actively looking for her, was driving him out of his mind.

Auggie stood across the room, the anger and dissatisfaction on his face evident. Dane knew how he'd feel if it were Emmy that was missing and his worry and irritation would mirror Auggie's.

Crime scene tape had been hung, sectioning off the back area and an officer stood watch making sure no unauthorized person went in or came out. He and Auggie were not allowed back there and he wasn't permitted to leave this spot, either. It was maddening to sit here helplessly. Wherever she was, she needed help and the two people who could help her most, were stuck in this fucking library, unable to do shit about it.

Auggie was finally allowed to approach him and they walked to a corner to chat. Most of the parents and their children had been authorized to leave, including his mom and Emmy. Of course, Stan was with them and he felt mildly relieved that they had someone with them.

"Dane, no training in the world could prepare me for this."

"I know what you mean, Auggie."

"But, I just can't sit here and do nothing. These cops are doing their jobs, but when I try to tell them I might have someone seeking revenge against me, they tell me to go to the station when I'm able to leave here and make a statement. We don't have fucking time for that."

He nodded. "I agree. I'm about ready to jump out of my skin. The wheels of justice are slow."

"So, do you have some friends who you can call upon to help out? I have one or two I can count on to assist us."

"Yes, I have one man I know and trust to keep things quiet, do his job and do it well." And he did, his best friend, Captain David Ferrance.

"As soon as they let us leave, call him and meet at my house at 1100 hours. I've got a plan."

Looking at his watch that gave him an hour to call on his best friend, the only man he knew without a doubt he could trust.

"Roger that. Who are you calling?"

Auggie didn't hesitate. "First and foremost, Richard Masters."

Hope started to rise. "Okay, I don't know him, but that will make four of us for certain."

"That's perfect. Let's not let anyone else in right now."

An officer approached, "Mr. Vickers, you're cleared to leave."

"Thanks. I'll see you in a bit, Dane."

Auggie's retreating back gave him hope that he'd be out there calling his man, and planning their next move.

He saw an officer walk from the back area with an evidence bag and Keirnan's necklace in it. He closed his eyes and sent up a silent prayer she was alright. But his gut and Auggie's call told him something had happened in Auggie's past that was coming back to haunt him and Keirnan was being used as the pawn.

Twenty minutes later an officer approached him. "Mr. Copeland, you are cleared to leave, but don't leave the area."

"Thank you." He breathed a sigh of relief and walked as quickly as he could to his truck, inside his first call was to David.

"Dave, I need some help. Likely outside the legal lines. But, I wouldn't ask if it wasn't important."

His friend, true to his dedication didn't hesitate. "Can I ask how far outside the lines?"

Dane took a deep breath. "Keirnan is missing. I think someone took her from the back of the library during a very busy time, so we're dealing with someone bold, dangerous and who wants to get attention in a big way. Auggie got a call telling him he'd pay for his past sins with his daughter's life."

"Fuck."

"Fuck is right. Local police are on the scene, but fuck Dave while they're doing their jobs they are s-l-o-w. In the meantime, Keirnan could be in the hands of a deranged asshole bent on some revenge that I know nothing about and doing who knows what to her."

"Fuck."

He heard Dave take a deep breath. "What do you need me to do?"

"We're meeting at 1100 hours at Auggie Vickers' house to set up a plan."

"I'm there for you. And Keirnan."

"Thanks."

"Text me the address."

Letting out a deep breath his next call was to his mom to update her and check on Emmy; Emmy had naturally been upset when he told her Keirnan got lost, he wasn't sure what else to say and didn't want to scare her senseless.

Then, he'd go over to Auggie's house early and get himself ready for whatever mission Auggie had in store for them. First order of business would be for Auggie to figure out who he had pissed off and what had happened which would hopefully give them a lead on where to find Keirnan. They could do this. They had to do this.

Glancing at the time on his phone, it had been three and a half hours since he'd noticed Keirnan missing. Four hours at most that she'd been gone, if whoever took her did so right away, which was likely. Four hours was long enough to do serious damage, but whoever did this also wanted to drag it out. He could only hope he was wrong.

Driving up Auggie's street, he saw the lights off in many of the houses, since it was close to 11:00 p.m. that wasn't uncommon.

He pulled into the driveway, took in a deep breath, and sent up a silent prayer that Keirnan was alive and well; though likely scared, and maybe traumatized, they'd get her back. He jumped from his truck and walked to the front door. Auggie swung it open before he hit the top step.

"Glad you're here. Come in."

"We need to talk about who has a vendetta against you and why."

"I agree. After talking with Richard on the phone I have it narrowed down to a couple of suspects.

They walked into the kitchen, Elaine stood in the corner by the coffee pot looking dazed, her eyes rimmed in red from recent tears and he hoped the next tears she shed were happy ones.

He walked to her and she wrapped her arms around his waist, laid her head on his chest and cried a few more tears. Through her crying, she said, "Get my baby back."

He hugged her and whispered in her ear, "I'll die trying."

She sobbed some more, and he simply stood with her in his arms and sent up another prayer that he would be successful.

## 26

Locating the door or what she thought was the door based on the size and feel of it, she ran her hands along both edges, locating the side with the hinges. Once she found it her hands ran across the door to the knob, and, of course, it was locked. Running her hands up the side with the knob, she was also disappointed to find a thrown deadbolt lock. She felt momentarily defeated and slid to the floor.

Once on the floor, she realized the bluish light in the room came from under the doorway, though faint, it allowed her to make out shapes and shadows, which was how she'd found the shelves that freed her earlier. Trying to ignore the creeps she felt about moving around in a dark damp basement or room, she inhaled and told herself to buck up; then she was immediately sorry she'd inhaled so deeply, the musty air filled her lungs and she coughed. Petrified of making any noise she quickly covered her coughing in the crook of her arm.

There had to be something in here she could use as a weapon the next time someone entered this room. It dawned on her, if they saw she'd gotten free of her restraints, they might tie her up tighter with something else or drug her so she was unconscious. Scrambling back to where she'd dumped the duct tape, she smoothed it out as much as she could to lay them over her wrists and ankles, so when they came back it would appear that she was still tied up.

While peeling the tape from itself, she heard a far door open then close and quickly wrapped the tape around her ankles, then her wrists, praying it looked tight enough.

She sat down where they'd dumped her, her head still foggy from the drug or inhalant they'd used to subdue her, but the adrenaline was helping her to metabolize it quickly which was a bonus.

Footsteps now sounded on the floor near the door and her heartbeat throbbed at an alarming rate and the thrumming in her ears threatened to drown out any other sound. She closed her eyes and took a deep breath, held it for a few moments then let it out slowly in an effort to calm herself. Not that it helped much.

Keeping her breathing even she stared in the direction of the door, hoping she'd get a chance to run. The jingling of keys reached her ears, then the keys sliding into the locks, two clicks and the door was opened, and light flooded the room, which hurt her eyes. Closing them briefly, she opened them again and stared at her captor in horror as she saw he was large and wearing a black ski mask. The fact that he didn't want her to see him scared the shit out of her and her heart pounded painfully in her chest.

"Eyes down." His gravelly voice commanded.

Looking at her hands laying in her lap and swallowing

rapidly to calm herself further, she tried talking to him in hopes he'd see her as a human.

"My name is Keirnan Vickers. Can you tell me why I'm here?"

"Shut up."

His body came closer, blocking the light from the hallway. He bent down, roughly grabbed her by the front of her sweater and pulled her to her feet. It hurt where the sweater bunched up under her arms; the tears she heard in the material angered her then scared her at the brutality of this man. Bending over, he shoved his shoulder into her stomach, though painful she kept her arms together as if her wrists were bound tightly when pinned between his shoulder and her body. He turned and hauled her from the darkened room, carrying her down a long hallway. She looked around trying to figure out where they were and how they'd gotten here. She had no memory of a car ride, but then she remembered she was hit on the side of her head at the library and she lost consciousness.

Nothing in the hallway, which was lit, or any items in it were recognizable. She'd been hoping she was still in the library and it was only a matter of time before Dane found her and saved her. No way to know how much time had passed. She tried to fight passing out from her inability to breathe, so, she focused on taking shallow breaths until they got to wherever this brute was taking her.

Finally they turned a corner into another, but smaller, room which was also dimly lit, but didn't smell as musty as the other one. Less frightening conditions right now and she'd take any relief she could get. He bent to set her on her feet, his big paws holding onto her by the front of her sweater again, he then pulled a chair forward and pushed her down onto it. His hand slid down over her left breast, gave it a squeeze, then he chuckled before pulling a roll of duct tape from a carabiner on his belt and unrolling long strips of the tape.

He reached down to grab her hands and she bolted from the chair, hoping like hell the tape around her legs hadn't resealed. She tripped slightly as the tape let loose, but her fear kept her upright. Thank God.

Making it through the door she instantly decided not to go in the direction they came from and turned to her right where she ran smack into the solid chest of another man. His iron grip tightened on each of her forearms and squeezed tightly.

"Just where in the fuck do you think you're going, Vickers?"

Unable to hold back the tears she started crying, her emotions at an all-time high. The first man in the ski mask grabbed her by her hair and pulled her away from the second man whom she'd not been able to see. One of his strong arms wrapped around her chest, her hair let loose, he pulled her back into the room; the blurring from her tears and the darkness rendering her unable to see the second man.

Being tossed roughly onto the wooden chair once again, the first man wasted no time in pulling her arms forcefully back behind her causing her to cry out. He wrapped the tape around her wrists and to the back of the chair, so she'd have no way to rip it apart unless a miracle happened.

He then roughly grabbed her left leg and pulled it over the side of the chair and taped her ankle to the leg. The tightness was terribly agonizing, but not as much as when he then brutally pulled her right leg over the other side of the chair, leaving her legs spread wide open, her ankles taped to the chair legs.

Terror such as she'd never experienced set in, panic rising at breakneck speed. Before she could have a coherent thought, the first big man used his knife to cut the top of her pretty sweater, and his rough hands ripped it open down the front, leaving her upper body exposed. Vomit rose so fast from her stomach, it spewed out of her mouth with force onto the man before her, which earned her another slap on the side of her head so hard her ear rang.

The last thing she heard was, "Get the camera turned on."

## 27

H e sat at the table with Auggie, folders on the table unopened. Auggie's blue eyes showed his tiredness and the faint red rims similar to those of his wife were a telltale sign he'd shed some tears, too. This made Dane's commitment even stronger than moments ago.

"Who do you think has her, Auggie?" He kept his voice even, trying not to sound panicked, but he was and there was no denying it.

"Back a few years ago, I'd say seven or eight, I completed a mission in the outskirts of New York. During that mission, a local town was used to shield the gun running activities of a homegrown terrorist group. Most of the townsfolk knew of some of the activities of the group, but went about their business as if nothing were going on out of fear for themselves and their families. Some were involved in it.

The leader of that group, a man who went by the name of Charles Watson, had set up a stronghold in the town square building, which operated as a bank. They had set up tunnels under the safe, which was sealed at night, allowing them all the privacy they needed to plan their takeover. During the day, they would leave through a backdoor of the bank and go to work at their various places of business, except for a certain few of the closest advisors.

Money was funneled to them through the bank tunnels, it was left in a special place in the safe at night where they could access it. This funded their operation. Our intel told us that local businesses, churches and minor political factions were where the money came from. Also a few foreign governments who wanted the President out of office.

We set up a coup, and waited for the day when they actually set their plans in motion. They left the bank in the early morning, after the safe opened, and began staking out various places around the town square where the President planned to be campaigning for the next election. Our mission was to catch them in the act of trying to assassinate the President, but above all else, prevent it. It meant we had to have our timing down perfectly. I had twenty men on my team. In the process of setting up the morning of the campaign speech, one of my guys accidentally detonated one of his IEDs, which killed two family members of Watson. I didn't think one of them was a daughter though. I've got Masters checking on the facts about that."

He listened as Auggie explained how he was in this predicament and as much as he wanted to know this, he just wanted Keirnan safe and in his arms. Time, this was all taking too much time, but he had to remember his training. Blasting in anywhere unprepared would get her killed and that wouldn't do at all. It didn't stop his guts from rolling though.

"Tell me about the other guy."

Auggie flipped the folder for Watson closed and opened the second folder.

"Mitchell Maklin is a home boy. Born and raised in California, he's a born troublemaker. In and out of juvie his entire life, his father absent, his mother worked two jobs to try and pay the bills but that meant she wasn't home. Maklin was home with his two siblings, both younger, both brothers. They were all in trouble. Stealing from local businesses and fighting with anyone who would fight. Maklin got into boxing when he was about 17, but could never break out because he carried a huge chip on his shoulder.

My unit encountered him when he'd kidnapped, and ra..."

Auggie swallowed several times and Dane knew what he'd been about to say, Maklin raped someone. That didn't sit well with either of them. Dane's gut dropped as his heart hammered. Sweat formed on his forehead as the clock on the wall behind Auggie sounded louder than it had before. Time. How much did they have left? What torture had Keirnan suffered already?

"Anyway," Auggie continued. "We were called in because he'd broken onto a military base and stole weapons and ammo. The woman he held hostage was a soldier on duty that night. After a day of hearing her screams as he beat her and raped her, they called in our specialty unit. It was part training mission for my team and all rescue."

He cleared his throat and picked up his coffee cup that said Army Dad on it. Sipping slowly, then setting it gently on the table, he wrapped both hands around the cup.

"Were you successful?"

He cleared his throat again. "We were, but what we didn't know was that Maklin had kids with him. Our intelligence told us they were his nephew and niece. During the rescue operation, the niece was too close to one of our explosives as we blew open the door; she was killed. The nephew was fatally shot. Maklin was nowhere to be found when we got there."

"Where did he take the soldier he kidnapped?"

"He stayed on base. It was the strangest thing. He'd scoped it all out beforehand, and found a small area on the base that was closed off to all personnel. He stayed right there."

Auggie's phone pinged and he picked it up off the table, read the text, tears in his eyes, he tapped once on the phone, then started crying.

Dane reached over and gently took the phone from his hand and saw the picture that had Auggie crumbling.

There sat Keirnan, taped to a chair, her upper body naked, her eyes blackened and smeared with her makeup, her chin and torso covered in what looked like vomit, her head being held up by her hair, a large bruise forming on the left side of her face, her legs spread open but, thank God, she still had her pants on. Hopefully she hadn't been raped so that maybe they had a little time to get to her before she was.

His breathing became stilted, coming in rasps like there was a boulder on his chest. His heart felt heavy and as though it would stop beating at any time and his eyes blurred. Sweet, kind, beautiful Keirnan was suffering for something she didn't do or understand. He was going to figure this out posthaste. No matter how many men did this to her, he would find them, and they would regret it. So, help him God.

---

## 28

"My gut tells me, Maklin." Dane whispered it.

"That's what my gut tells me, too." Auggie choked out.

A knock sounded at the front door and Auggie stood, but Elaine had rushed from the living room and opened it. She flew into the arms of the man he assumed was Richard Masters as he softly comforted her with words of assurance that they would do whatever was necessary to bring Keirnan home.

They moved into the house as David appeared behind them, then looked into the kitchen to see him sitting at the table with Auggie. He stood and as he neared his best friend, tears sprang to his eyes. What was it about seeing someone you trusted and, yes, loved like a brother, to bring out all the emotions you were trying to hold at bay?

He hugged his friend, probably the hardest he'd ever hugged him, then stepped back. Swiping the moisture from his eyes he looked into his friend's green eyes and shook his head. Softly, he said, "I'm terrified."

"I know, I could hear it in your voice."

"Come on in and meet Auggie." He stopped quickly as he saw Elaine, suddenly a bit ashamed that he'd just invited his friend in as if it were his own place. She stepped forward and reached out her hand.

"I'm Elaine Vickers, Keirnan's mother, and this is a very good friend of ours, Major Richard Masters."

David introduced himself, hands were shaken, and they were ushered to the kitchen, where introductions were made once again.

Masters had a satchel over his shoulder, which Dane hadn't seen previously. Once he began pulling papers from it, it was a sight to behold.

Masters wasted no time. "My eye is on Maklin. The girl that was killed wasn't his niece, it was his daughter. The mother and he were estranged, and he never made a claim to the girl legally because he didn't want to be on the hook for child support. But, DNA testing was done after the kidnapping and rape and it was determined both children were his and the mother had reported them missing just hours before Maklin's daughter was killed. The mother then identified the boy at the hospital."

"Son of a bitch," Auggie said.

The papers were passed around and it dawned on him that sometimes people like this repeated their actions.

"If he stayed right where he kidnapped the female soldier in some closed off area on the base, suppose he found a similar closed off place in the library and then located a cellar or unknown basement or tunnels under the library? Maybe he has her there. It fits his M.O."

Auggie glanced up at him, and nodded. "You could be onto something there. But the local police should have checked for that."

David then chimed in, "I have a friend who's on the

local police force, she works as a dispatcher. Let me see if she can access something for me."

David walked away as he pulled his phone from his back pocket. Dane watched him walk toward the front door and was so grateful he'd called him.

Masters and Auggie kept talking about their mission. Some things that seemed important about the last time and Auggie tapped his phone a couple of times then quickly handed it over to Masters who looked at the picture of Keirnan. His jaw tightened, and he swallowed a few times, his blue eyes glistened as they began filling with tears then he set the phone on the table, screen side down.

Masters quickly picked the phone up again and spread his fingers over the screen to enlarge the photo. His eyes focused on something and without a word he turned the phone to him.

Dane's eyes focused on the object, which looked like it was just behind Keirnan's right shoulder. It appeared to be a photograph, an old one and it looked just like the founder of the library. The same picture that Keirnan had told him she hated because it seemed as if his eyes were following her.

"They're there. At the library." His heart raced. She was there. She was close.

Masters took the phone back and began examining the picture all around the background looking for anything that would give them an idea of where Keirnan was.

"I see the corner of a window, though it looks boarded up," he said.

David came back to the kitchen and shook his head. "Cops are still on the scene; she tried calling the sergeant on duty and he said he didn't have time to talk to crack-pots calling in tips right now. She's supposed to screen them with the officer who is there."

"Bekah." He just happened to think about her. "Keirnan has told me that Bekah, the curator, knows that place like the back of her hand. She may know if there is a cellar or tunnels or something below the library. She also may know where the original drawings or blueprints are. They should show whatever is under that building."

He called the library, thrilled that Keirnan had him save the number in his phone last week. The phone rang and rang and he was about to give up hope when finally a breathless voice answered, "Friday Harbor Library."

"Bekah?" His stomach tightened as he waited for her to respond.

"Yes, this is she. Who am I speaking to?"

"Dane Copeland. Keirnan's boyfriend."

"Any word, Dane? I'm so worried for her."

"No, not yet. Are the cops still there?"

"Most of them have left, but the sergeant and two others are still here collecting evidence."

He didn't know if that was good or not. "Listen, Bekah, do you know if there is a basement in that building or a cellar or any type of tunnel system below?"

She was silent for a while. "I've never seen one, but the librarian before me told me it was part of the under-ground railroad back in the day when slavery was still legal. There must be some system down there or false walls."

"Do you have blueprints or any old documents that might give us a lead?"

"I'd have to go and pull them from the file cabinets in

the back. I'm not sure if the officers will allow me to do that."

Hopefully they'd want to find Keirnan as badly as they did. "Can you check, please, and call me back." He gave her his phone number and hung up, hoping she'd be successful.

"I have to go the library. I think we're on to something and we need to be there if Bekah finds anything that might give us a lead."

## 29

D avid insisted on driving and he had to admit, he was glad for it. The whole drive he'd hardly paid attention to the route at all. As soon as his thoughts went to what Keirnan might be going through, he forced himself to think of the moment he'd hold her in his arms again. He just had to believe he would and whatever torment she was going through, he'd help her heal. For the first time since Catherine, he felt like he had a future to believe in aside from being Emmy's dad and he wanted Keirnan in it. He hoped in all of his years of risky missions, bringing home soldiers and Marines who'd been captured and worse, that he'd been sympathetic to the families who waited at home for their loved ones to return. Being on this end of it felt like a slow torture. How did families have the strength to persist when their loved ones were gone for years?

A quick shake of his head to clear those thoughts caught his friend's attention.

"We'll find her, Dane; we won't stop till we do."

Swallowing the large knot in his throat, he could only

nod, afraid the trepidation would take hold if he said anything.

Pulling his cell phone from the side pocket in his dockers, he tapped the number for the local PD.

"Friday Harbor Police Department, how may I help you?"

"This is..." His voice sounded like a croak, so he cleared his throat and tried again. "This is Dane Copeland. Officers were called to the Friday Harbor library this evening for a missing person. I have reason to believe that she's in the building or in a basement area or cellar. I'd like to speak to the officer in charge, please."

"Let me see if I can get through to him, Mr. Copeland."

Turning into the parking lot of the library, there were only two cruisers left and a lone white Jeep on the far edge, which he assumed was Bekah's. Pulling to a stop at the far-right edge of the lot, Dane watched Masters pull in alongside them. Auggie was in what appeared to be a heated conversation. Masters jumped from the driver's side and walked toward them. Dane and David both opened their doors and exited the truck.

"Auggie is trying to call in some favors for assistance from the military base, but has only butted up against wall after wall."

David replied, "Dane's trying to get through to the officer in charge."

Finally a few clicks could be heard on the phone and a male voice came on. "Officer McNally."

"Officer McNally, this is Dane Copeland. Keirnan's father received a text from Keirnan's kidnapper with a picture of her tied up and beaten. " His voice broke and he inhaled to regain his composure. "We believe she's in the library somewhere. A picture of Mr. Vandebrooke is hanging in the background."

"There are pictures of Mr. Vandebrooke all over town, he practically built every building in town."

"The same picture as the one hanging in the back room?"

"A few of them are different but..."

"Look we're here, please, let us come in and show you the picture and let us help you find her."

There was a long pause, muffled conversation and a couple of clicks on the line.

"I'll be out to meet you in the parking lot."

The line went dead, and frustration bubbled up inside of him. That was frustration, mixed with a heavy dose of anger drizzled with fear. They were wasting time.

A truck door slammed and Auggie stalked over to them.

"Military can't get involved. I figured that would be the answer, but dammit, I thought I could get some assistance."

The front door to the library opened and a stocky figure in a police uniform cautiously approached them.

"Who do I have here?" He asked before getting halfway to them.

Dane stepped forward. "Dane Copeland. These are my friends, David and Richard and Keirnan's father, Auggie."

The cop nodded. "I'm Sergeant McNally."

Dane glanced at Auggie, "Show him the text, please."

Auggie still had his phone in his hand. Tapping a few times he pulled up the text and quickly handed the phone over without looking at the picture of Keirnan.

Dane's heart hammered in his chest as the seconds ticked by waiting for Sergeant McNally to say something.

Masters stepped forward and addressed the tired-looking cop.

"If you look at the picture behind her shoulder here," he pointed to the picture, "that's the picture of Vandebrooke I noticed."

Masters moved the picture with his finger, "There's what appears to be a boarded up window."

The Sergeant looked up from the phone. "We've been over the entire place. There's nothing here. We didn't find a basement or cellar."

Dane stepped forward. "This property was used as part of the underground railroad, there must be hidden halls or false walls. Please let us check. The curator likely has the plans somewhere in there. "

"I'm sorry, Mr. Copeland, I know you're anxious, but we aren't finished with our investigation yet, so I can't let you in. But, Mr. Vickers, I would like this text forwarded to me, please. We'll check it against anything we might have at the station."

Auggie took his phone from the Sergeant. "I have an idea who did this. Mitchell Maklin. He has my daughter. He intends to kill her because his daughter was killed on a mission I was involved in."

"I'll have you make a statement at the station, Mr. Vickers, so we can check everything out. Until then, we need to finish up here."

The Sergeant turned and quickly made his way back to the library and behind the safety of the big wooden doors. They likely gave off a dangerous vibe.

"Fuck that," Auggie spat. "We're going in on our own. We have the brain power, the years of experience and the sense of urgency to get this done. If it were his daughter in there, he'd move heaven and earth to find the secret ways into that building, I intend to do the same."

"Dane, call the curator again and see if she had any luck finding the blueprints or other information for us." Auggie commanded.

Nodding, he pulled his phone up, searched for Bekah's number and tapped the call icon. Listening as her phone rang, he grew more impatient with each ring. Finally she answered. "This is Bekah."

"Bekah, Dane Copeland. Have you had any luck finding the blueprints to help us get into the basement area of the building?

## 30

Cold air blew down on her bare skin. She couldn't see from where; her eyes were swollen from the multiple punches she'd suffered. Her arms were numb, her fingers, too. Her legs and feet were the same. The only thing she felt, right now, where she could, was pain. And cold.

She slowly lifted her head and the throbbing increased. Her ears were ringing on both sides now from a further slap, and her throat was parched. Licking her lips did little good, her mouth, too, was dry as dust. But, at least for the moment, she was alone in this wretched room.

She didn't know the second man who taunted her and hit her. He had dark stringy hair. She'd never seen him before, but the first man wearing the mask, there was something familiar about him. And why would one of them wear a mask and the other not? It didn't make any sense.

Faint voices filtered into the room, from where she couldn't determine; she didn't even know where this room was other than down the hall from the dank, damp room she'd been taken at first.

When the masked man cut her sweater and bra from her, she sat exposed from the waist up. And, as humiliating as that was, when the second man turned the camera on her, that was even worse. Thank God, so far at least, they hadn't raped her, though the way they had her splayed open in this chair worried her to no end.

She tried wriggling her hands to loosen the tape, but they were bound tightly to the chair. Doing the same with her feet, she felt the right tape loosen just a bit and hope swarmed through her. Continuing to wriggle her foot around, she was able to position her right heel against the chair leg and stretch the tape a bit more, allowing her foot to move up and down. With any luck, she could saw the tape against the chair leg and free at least one leg, then she'd work on the other.

A few times up and down and she heard the tape begin to tear. As fast as she could move her foot, she felt a surge of energy flow through her and finally the tape split. The pain was immense, but once she could breathe normally, she started working on the other foot. She leaned over just a bit and realized if she could move up a bit, she'd be able to move her body to the side a little and saw the tape of each wrist on the chair back. Abandoning her left foot, she struggled as she twisted and moved as much as she was able, making little headway, but even the smallest movement was a measure of progress. The throbbing in her head increased as she exerted herself, but terror kept her going. Finally able to position herself so she could saw at the tape on the back of the chair, and add as much pressure as she could muster, she continued to work to free herself.

Stopping for just a second to make sure she wasn't drawing any attention, she listened through the ringing in her ears and could still hear the muffled voices. Inhaling as much air as she could into her lungs, she continued sawing on the tape at her wrists which was difficult and extremely painful. Something sharp dug into her right wrist and her breath caught at the pain. She could feel a trickle of what she assumed was blood drip down her right arm and at this point her only thought was if she bled enough, maybe she could slip through the tape. Moving her arms once again, she sawed away with all she had in her. She turned ever so slightly so that her blood might drip on her left wrist as well. The side of her right hand began to slip a bit in the tape and she almost cried with relief that this might work.

She felt the tape loosen but didn't have the strength in her arms to pull the tape open. With all of her tenacity, she began sawing once again, her left wrist loosening a bit as well. Not more than five times and her wrists fell free of their bonds. The pain of her arms and wrists falling forward was mixed with relief then fear and she began making fists and releasing them to regain feeling and movement in her fingers. The intense tingling sensation erupted throughout her arms, wrists and fingers as the blood began rushing forth through her veins. Inhaling and exhaling, she allowed herself a minute for the strong sensation to abate, then bent down to release her left foot from the tape. Trying at first to undo it from the tape end, fear began to grip her as little headway seemed to be made. Attempting to tear at the tape from the top edge, she used her finger nail to puncture a small tear in the top of the tape, then using her left foot for pressure against the tape, she continued to tear it down, freeing herself from the chair.

Standing while the feeling flooded into her legs and feet was difficult as she swayed or lost her balance. She frantically looked around for a way out. No doubt the door was locked so she didn't even bother to check it. Catching sight of the boarded window at the top of the wall farthest from the door, she quietly picked up the wooden chair that had held her prisoner for the past who knew how many hours and carried it to the window. Standing on it, she used the wall to brace herself as she gently pulled at the old wood covering. Excited to find the wood dry and easily breaking apart, she tugged small pieces of wood off the window, exposing it to the dim light in the room.

Once she had an opening big enough that she thought she could fit through, she glanced around the room for something to break it with. That's when she saw the camera still sitting on its tripod. Stepping down gingerly, not trusting her feet or legs to handle her weight, she limped to the tripod and grabbed it with the camera still attached.

Back to the window as quickly as she could go, she once again climbed onto the chair. Looking away and with as much force as she could muster, she hit the window with the legs of the tripod. The old brittle glass broke instantly and with minimal sound. Using the tripod legs, she continued gingerly breaking the glass from its frame, then running the legs along the window opening to remove small shards of the old glass. Not sure where it would lead her, she knew it was a better choice than where she was. The darkness on the other side of the window only told her it was either dark outside or dark in that next room. Hopefully, whoever had her held captive wouldn't be in there. Whoever they were.

Using her fingers for leverage, she tried lifting herself up to the window, but was unable to get a good grip on anything. Taking a deep breath, she looked around the room yet again for something to help her out of the window.

# 31

———

"Okay, listen up," Auggie said. "Dane, take the east side of the library. Rich, the north. David, the south and I'll take the west. Search everything, behind bushes and shrubs in case there's a boarded up window. Check anything that looks younger than a hundred years old. Doors, windows - everything. Make sure your weapons are loaded and ready."

Dane nodded and so did the others. "Let's sync up our phones and add each of us to a group message so we can easily keep in touch, put your phones on vibrate so we don't call attention to ourselves. Communication units would be better, but this is what we have."

They each took a couple of minutes to follow orders.

Auggie again directed the search. "Call in if you find anything, no matter how small. Let's go."

Walking to the east side of the building he had his phone out and the flashlight turned on and pointed at the ground. A clump of shrubs to his right and against the building caught his attention and he searched all around them for anything. Flashing his light against the building he didn't see any new or newer brick, no old windows and nothing boarded up. Trying to ignore the frustration that bubbled up, he pressed on. Flashing his light on the building to the top in case they were wrong about the basement/cellar idea yielded nothing. A new rose bush up ahead was his next target, but a thorough search showed him nothing of value.

His phone vibrated and he quickly looked at the caller's name. David.

Tapping the icon to dial his friend he asked, "What do you have?"

"If you're finished with your side, I could use some help over here."

"I'm almost finished. Be there soon."

Finishing his call, he continued along the east wall of the building; now eager to see what David had but knowing he needed to be thorough in his search. Forcing himself to look along the east wall, he completed his inspection disappointed at finding nothing, but hopeful David had. He hurried around to the south side of the building to find David looking at the ground about fifty feet from the building.

"What do you have?"

"Look at this, it's a dip in the ground in a straight line from the library building to this spot right here. If this had been used in the underground railroad, it's possible there is a tunnel under here, causing the ground to dip. So, I'm thinking, right here," He tapped his foot on the ground, which was bare, but there was a landscaped area just in front of it. "Could be a holding room and possibly an escape route for escaped slaves as they moved them hidden in carts and the like to take them to the next unseen safe stop."

"Okay. I'll go around to the right and begin searching in the landscaping for anything that might help."

"Roger."

Feeling hopeful anew, he shone his light on the ground looking for any signs that would be useful.

A raised section of the landscaping with a clump of Hydrangea bushes swaying in the slight breeze caught his attention. He couldn't see David but knew he was there. Moving along once more, he tripped over something protruding from the ground. Gaining his balance, he shone his light on the protrusion only to see a corner of a block of cement. Kicking his foot along the block to move the dirt, his heart raced when he found something. He began kicking furiously along the edge his hopes rising. Able to uncover the top and two sides of a block, he continued along to see if there was another one and perhaps a structure underneath.

"What the fuck?" He heard David say. His heart racing, he ran around to see what his friend had found.

Just before rounding the corner, gunshots sounded. "Shit, hang on." David said.

Pulling his weapon, Dane rounded the corner to see David pulling on a hand that had reached between the flowers in the landscaping.

"Don't let that bitch get away." A voice called from below.

More shots sounded, a woman screamed, and he knew it was Keirnan. Holstering his weapon, he reached down to the woman now emerging from a small hole and tugged her from the opening as his friend began shooting into the hole.

"Keirnan?" It was dark and he couldn't see her face clearly but her body, which he picked up and carried toward the front of the library felt like her.

"Dane?" Her voice was hopeful, the sound of it nearly crumbled him.

"Yes, I'm here baby."

Shallow sobs came from her body, but her arms wrapped around his neck and held tight.

"I think I'm shot in the leg. It burns."

"Okay, hang on and let me get you to safety."

More shots were fired, then he heard Auggie yell, "Don't let those fuckers get away."

He carried Keirnan to David's truck. "I need to set you down for just a minute while I open the tailgate. Which leg are you shot in?"

"My right." Her voice sounded stronger now and relief swam through him.

"Okay, Princess, stand on your right leg, but don't let go of me."

Gently setting her down on to her right leg, he reached forward and pulled David's tailgate down. Picking her up, he set her on the tailgate and watched as she grabbed the front of her cut open sweater to close it."

He quickly pulled his shirt off and slipped it over her head, helping her get her arms through the armholes.

"This will keep you covered, sweetheart."

"Thank you."

"Let me look at your leg."

She pulled her left leg up onto the tailgate as she twisted to the side. Her left hand never left his shoulder.

"They were going to kill me," she sobbed.

"They aren't going to, Princess. Your dad, Masters and my friend, David are all here to bring you home."

She started crying and he stopped for a moment to wrap his arms around her and hold her close.

He sniffed her hair, his right hand at the back of her head, holding her to him and both of her arms wrapped around his neck as she sobbed into his neck.

After a few moments, he hated saying it but he needed to make sure she wasn't shot in a vein, more than once or in some other dire way that needed immediate attention.

"Princess, I need to check your leg."

Her hold on him lessened and he pulled away. Picking his phone up off the tailgate, he turned on the flashlight. Handing it to Keirnan, "Hold this so I can open this side of your slacks and examine your leg."

She shakily held his phone as he ripped her pants up the side. She tried stifling a sob but he looked up at her tear-filled swollen eyes.

"I'll buy you a new pair, Princess."

She managed to choke out. "It's not that."

Shot in the upper thigh on her left leg, it had already stopped bleeding which meant no arterial damage. But no exit wound which meant the bullet was still lodged inside.

"Okay, as soon as David gets here to open the truck we'll get the first aid kit out and patch you up until an ambulance gets here."

"Okay."

"We aren't supposed to be here, Princess, so there's likely going to be charges pressed against us. And as I carried you away, I saw the cops investigating, running toward the shooting. So, they'll likely call 911 for you and they'll take you to the hospital, but the rest of us will surely be detained. I'll get to you as soon as I can, okay?"

"But you saved me."

"I know, honey, but unless Auggie can call in some favors, we're probably in the hot seat."

He dipped his head and kissed her lips. "Totally worth it though."

## 32

Keeping her brave face on, Keirnan only winced a couple of times as Dane checked her wound. Seeing her father's grief-stricken face come around the corner, as soon as his eyes landed on hers he raced forward and wrapped her in a bear-hug. She heard a sob come from deep in his chest and then his breathing deepened as he regained control.

"I'm so happy we have you back, baby. I'm so sorry."

"Don't worry, Daddy, I'll be fine. Just make sure you all don't go to jail."

"That's the next thing I need to take care of, baby."

She watched her father pull his phone from his pocket and tap a couple of times.

"Vickers here. I'm calling in a favor."

He retreated to sit inside Richard Masters' truck and she hoped he could get this worked out.

Dane stood by her side, his arm around her shoulders, his warmth a needed comfort.

"Put this on and stop showing off." A man, who she

assumed was his friend David, tossed Dane a sweatshirt he'd pulled from the back of his truck.

"Keirnan, I'm glad you're back with Dane and your family. My name is David Ferrance." He held his hand out to her and Dane said as his head poked through the neck of the sweatshirt he'd been given.

"That's Captain David Ferrance. He's modest. And truth be told, the women all call him Captain Fine Ass." Dane chuckled.

Captain Ferrance shot Dane the middle finger and both men laughed.

Richard Masters appeared around the truck.

"Okay, update. Auggie's calling in a couple of favors. Thank God, he's owed by so many people. The local police are on the scene of course, they came running when they heard shots. They're pulling the bodies from one of the rooms below ground, no one down there survived, or if they did, they're hiding. The police have called in more officers and we're to stay put until we're questioned. 911 has been called for you Keirnan."

"Thank you, Rich, I don't know how I'll ever be able to repay you for helping Dane and Dad get me. Especially if Dad can't call in enough favors."

"Keirnan, there's no need to thank me or repay me. I'd have helped your dad no matter and I know he'd have done the same for me. The fact that it's one of our own takes any hesitation out of the equation."

Dane reached forward with his hand extended and Rich shook it. Dane added, "I'm also at your service should you ever need anything, sir."

Rich nodded then turned to head back to where the police were gathered, David followed him. Dane returned to her side and perched himself on the tailgate at her hip, facing her. Using the flashlight from his phone, he examined her face, which in all the commotion she'd forgotten about, but now realized her eyes were swollen, her face was bruised from being punched, and her ears were still ringing. Her jaw was a bit sore as well and vanity kicked in and she realized she must look horrible. Covering her face with both of her hands she heard him take a deep breath as his hands pulled hers away.

"Don't hide yourself from me, Princess."

"I must look a fright."

"You look alive, a bit the worse for wear, but alive and that's what matters more than anything. You'll heal, which is the main thing, and, in a few days, this will all be behind us."

"I hope you're right, Dane. Who are those men and why did they want to kill me?"

"Your dad needs to explain that, Princess. I don't know that I have the full story, I just knew we had to get you back."

Her heart hammered in her chest. She was falling in love with this man and that scared her as much as thrilled her. Just having him carry her away from her prison cell was enough to make her swoon. But, the concern in his expression, the care in his fingers as he touched areas that must have been turning colors on her face, it was all eliminating any doubt in a relationship with Dane that she may have once had. Not that she'd had any, but she had counseled herself to take it easy and not get too wrapped up. They also had Emersyn to think about.

The sirens from the ambulance and additional officers reached their ears and Dane smiled as he reminded her. "I'll likely not be able to come with you. I'll try, but may not be allowed. How about I call your mom and have her meet you at the hospital so you aren't alone?"

She tried to smile, but it hurt, so she nodded. "That would be wonderful. I'm feeling a bit paranoid."

He nodded. "It'll take a while for that to go away, but we'll work on it together. Now, give me your mom's number."

She did as he asked and watched his face as he spoke to her mom, but his eyes never left hers and that was comforting in itself.

The ambulance pulled into the library parking lot. He waved them over to their location and then all the commotion began. People hovered around her, both EMTs and police officers. She could hear Dane asking to come with her and an officer telling him he needed to be questioned and stay put. Dane glanced her way and winked and just that small gesture made her feel a thousand times better. Then she saw an officer come to talk to him; she was loaded into the back of the ambulance and that was the last she saw of Dane.

## 33

Watching as the ambulance pulled out of the parking lot with Keirnan in the back made his gut drop and fill with dread. He'd have given anything to go with her, to make sure she felt safe. After what she'd been through it would be awhile before she felt safe again, that was a fact. PTSD was real and it was harder for some to overcome than others. He'd have to talk to her to find out what she needed and he or Auggie would hook her up with a good psychologist to help her through it all. He meant what he said, too, he'd help her through it all.

"Mr. Copeland, I need to take your statement."

"Okay."

"Tell me what you were doing here after you'd been released from our hold earlier this evening."

He told his story, without naming names, just saying they'd all decided to come and see if they could find the hidden tunnels they knew were here. The officers on duty were doing all they could, but he felt time was of the essence as they'd seen the picture and Auggie believed this was revenge through and through. No sense in lying at this point, their stories needed to match now more than ever. They'd shown the lead investigator her picture, it was all on a report now or soon would be.

After what felt like hours, he was released until it was determined whether charges would be brought; and he wasn't to leave the area until he heard from them. Since he had Emmy they didn't consider him a flight risk and Auggie did manage to get some sway with the Chief of Police by calling in some of his favors, but he wasn't sure how much sway that would be.

He was so tired at this point all he wanted to do was go home and sleep, but he needed to go to the hospital and see how Keirnan was doing. She'd been through so much today, and those bruises on her face were likely only going to darken and become more painful as the night wore on. The bullet in her leg didn't seem to have hit anything vital, but he wasn't a surgeon and she needed one to remove the bullet.

Pulling into the hospital parking lot, he sighed heavily before opening the door. Stepping down from his truck he walked to the hospital entrance and made his way to the reception desk.

"How may I help you, sir?" The overly perky young woman asked him.

"Keirnan Vickers. She was brought in earlier with a gunshot wound to the leg. Is she out of surgery and recovery?"

The woman's fingers flew over the keys of a keypad and within a few seconds, she said, "Room 484. I'm not able to tell you anything more."

He nodded, too tired to even say thanks, and took off in the direction of the elevators. The slow methodical hum of the motor nearly put him to sleep as the elevator's warmth felt like a hug.

With a slight swish the doors opened, and he stepped off on the fourth floor. The last time he'd been in a hospital was when Catherine had died. The chills that ran the length of his body now woke him up and left a hot rock in the pit of his stomach and a touch of sorrow in his heart. His eyes took in everything. The nurses, the color of sickly green on the walls of the hospital, the room numbers posted at each door along the corridor, the machines sitting outside of various rooms, the empty gurneys parked against the walls, the quiet beeping of heart monitors and hissing of the oxygen machines helping other patients breathe. He hated it all.

Turning the corner to the left he looked for 484 and felt relief mixed with a bit of trepidation at what he'd find when he walked in. Stopping outside of her door, he took in a deep breath and slowly let it out before silently pushing on the door to peek inside.

Elaine, Keirnan's mom, sat in a recliner facing the bed, her sleeping form listing to the left, making it look uncomfortable. Turning his head he found Keirnan, asleep, a pulse ox meter monitor clipped to her right fore-finger, a blood pressure cuff on her right arm and a couple of different IV's dripping into her left arm. The bruising on her face was now very prominent and his stomach rolled at what she'd gone through during her hours with those homicidal assholes.

Walking to her right side, he looked down at her and watched her chest rise and fall in a steady rhythm and contented himself with the fact that she was sleeping easy. After the surgery to remove the bullet, she was no doubt sedated to get through the night.

Glancing around the room he found another chair against the wall in front of the window, softly made his way there, and sat as quietly as he could. The fabric made a noise and Elaine's head popped up, but he put his finger to his lips then settled back, moving his gaze to make sure he didn't wake Keirnan.

Elaine smiled at him. Before he could take another breath the door opened and Auggie walked in and straight to his daughter's side, doing the same thing he just did, making sure she was resting comfortably.

Nodding at him, Auggie then turned to his wife and motioned for her to come outside with him. She stood and followed him to the door. As badly as he wanted to know what Elaine knew about Keirnan's condition, he also didn't want to leave her and didn't want to interrupt their private moment. He'd find out tomorrow.

Stretching his legs out in front of him, he slumped down in the chair, rested his head against the wall, reached out to hold Keirnan's hand in his, then closed his eyes. Sleep came easy.

## 34

The movements of someone in her room startled her awake and she bolted upright, her heart hammering in her chest. Blinking her eyes into focus, a sweet-faced nurse rushed to her and whispered, "It's okay, hon. I'm just checking your monitors. How are you feeling?"

Letting out a long breath to calm herself she laid back in bed and blinked away the moisture that gathered in her eyes.

"I'm fine. You scared me is all."

A deep male voice said, "Don't be scared, Princess, I'm here with you."

Her head spun to the left to see Dane, righting himself in the chair, which seemed far too small for him to sleep in and not comfortable in the slightest.

"Did you sleep there?"

Sliding his hands down his face he huffed out, "Yeah. Sort of."

"Oh, Dane, you didn't need to do that. I thought Mom was here."

He stood and stretched. "She was when I got here, then your dad came and checked in. I fell asleep, so I don't know if they left then or came back in after they had a moment to chat."

Pulling his phone from his pocket he checked the time and saw that it was 5:00 a.m. Emmy would be up soon.

He stood next to the bed and took her hand in his. "How are you this morning?"

"I'm good."

She touched the side of her face. "How purple am I?"

He grinned at her, brushed the back of his fingers down the side of her puffy face, so gentle it didn't hurt.

"The most stunning shade I've ever seen. Of course, you wear it well."

She giggled which hurt, she'd been a punching bag just yesterday, causing her to hold the left side of her face. "Please, you don't need to lie, I won't crumble."

He leaned in and touched his lips to hers softly, then stood and said, "I'd never lie to you."

The nurse sighed, and said to Keirnan, "Wow, you've got a keeper there."

She shyly replied, "I think so, too."

Dane's tired smile and wink made her feel much better than just a moment ago.

"I've got to call mom and tell her what happened last night and see if she can get Emmy to school today. I'll be right back."

"Hey,..." He stopped to look at her and she swallowed.

"Do you mind calling her from here so I can hear everything? I don't know all that happened yet."

He smiled at her and it made the gloom go away. She felt almost panicky that he'd leave and while she hated being clingy, she worried that one of those men would come for her.

"Sure." He pulled his phone from his pocket, then walked back to the bed and perched on the edge of it. As he pulled up his mom's number, Auggie and Elaine walked into the room.

"Good morning, Sunshine," Elaine said brightly.

They came to Keirnan's bedside and Elaine's worried eyes fell on Keirnan's face. She gently touched the bruises on her daughter's face and her eyes filled with tears.

"Oh, honey, I'm so sorry. How do you feel this morning? How is your leg?"

"Sore. But I'm relieved."

Auggie's voice cracked with emotion when he finally spoke. "Baby, I'm so sorry you got caught up in something that was meant for me. I'll never be able to forgive myself."

"Oh, Daddy, please don't carry a ton of guilt, you had no way of knowing there were apparently two deranged men out there looking to do you harm."

Her father's eyes filled with moisture and all he could do was nod.

Dane said, "I was just getting ready to call my mom and tell her what was going on. Can you update us as to all that transpired last night?"

Taking a deep breath, then clearing his throat, Auggie replied, "Absolutely."

"The bullet nicked your femur so you'll be sore, but the doctors felt no permanent damage was done. Though you may feel it when the weather is especially damp or changing. It was removed and the damaged tissue stitched up. They'll be getting you up and walking today. The bruises on your face..." Auggie cleared his throat and swallowed a few times and her heart hurt for the guilt her father was carrying. "The bruises will heal and you don't have any broken bones, thank God."

He turned his gaze to back to her. "The two men who had you in the cellar room were Curtis Daniels and..." He hesitated for a moment and she thought her heart would explode at the silence that fell over them.

"Daniel Murphy."

She gasped and sucked in a deep breath and held it. Slowly she let it out then said, "As in Principal Murphy? My boss?"

"Yes. We're still not sure of the connection between Daniels and Murphy and why they were bent on getting even with me through you. I had thought it was someone else entirely. Both men are dead, shot during your rescue. You're safe now baby girl, and I'm so very sorry."

The air whooshed from her lungs and she settled back onto her pillow. Stunned wouldn't even come close to how she felt about this news.

"I don't understand Principal Murphy doing me harm. He always spoke to me when..." She froze. The man with the mask, she thought he seemed familiar in some way. Thinking on it now that's probably why he wore a mask.

"He didn't want me to see him," she mumbled.

"What does that mean, Keirnan?" her father asked.

"Principal Murphy. He didn't want me to know it was him. At first, they kept me in a room like a basement. There were metal shelves in there and it was damp and musty smelling. I cut the tape around my wrists and ankles and got loose. I made the mistake of pretending I was still bound when he came in to get me. He wore a mask, but picked me up and threw me over his shoulder. I didn't recognize him, but later, after they taped me to the chair." She swallowed and waited to regain her quickly fading composure. She inhaled deeply and swallowed again. Dane squeezed her hand and she looked into his beautiful eyes and felt stronger.

He leaned closer and whispered, "It's okay, Princess."

"I thought he seemed familiar. I couldn't place him, and honestly if my life depended on it, I wouldn't have thought it was him anyway."

Dane squeezed her hand gently again and she looked at him and tried to smile, but her swollen face probably only looked creepy when she did. But, he smiled at her, winked and nodded his head.

Dane then turned to her father, "Auggie, do you have any news on our status?"

## 35

He was hopeful it would all work out, after all, they didn't hamper the police investigation, they completed it. But, they did it by skirting the law, so there could be consequences. Honestly, time was wasting away while the police department had to follow the rules and do things by the book.

Auggie responded. "I have a friend in the military, higher up, working with the local PD to smooth things over. He knows the police chief and is singing our praises and negotiating on our behalf. We should know something by today."

Nodding, he then looked at Keirnan, her poor bruised and swollen face a testament to what she'd recently been through. To say he was relieved that she was once again safe would be a gross understatement. The instant he'd realized something had happened to her; he'd been gripped by near panic. His heart squeezed so tightly he didn't know how it would continue to beat.

He kissed the hand he was holding, then said, "I have to call Mom. I'll be right back."

She nodded, tried to smile, but it looked more like a grimace. He nodded at Auggie and Elaine, then walked to the door and stepped into the hallway. He made his way to the room they called the family room, and was relieved to find it empty. Walking to the large wall of windows he pulled his phone out and tapped his mom's picture. Holding his phone to his ear he looked out over the parking lot and the sea of cars and trucks parked there. Even at this hour of the morning vehicles were entering and exiting the lot and he wondered where all of these people were going at such an early hour. Likely a shift change of some sort.

"Dane, how are you and how is Keirnan?" His mother's worried voice sounded over the phone.

"She's fine. Surgery removed the bullet, it nicked her femur, but praise the Lord, it didn't shatter it. She's bruised badly, but she'll heal. The most important thing will be for her to feel safe again. To deal with the likely PTSD that she'll experience. We'll get her help for that."

"Oh, praise be that she's okay. That poor beautiful girl. I'm glad you stayed with her last night."

"Me, too. How's Emmy?"

He heard his mom take a deep breath. "She was better after I told her that Keirnan was safe. I didn't say anything about her being shot, but she slept with me last night. She was scared and kept asking if some bad man would come and take her, too."

Gut punched. That's what that felt like. The thought of his little girl in the hands of some monster made his blood boil. And that's when he realized how Auggie must be feeling. Helpless. Responsible. A rage like no other. And guilty he wasn't with her when she'd been so scared. Thank God for his mom.

Seeing a white car pull into the lot at the far corner, he watched as it crawled through the parking lot, slowly gliding down one lane, then the next, then the next. It went past empty parking spaces but was methodically maneuvering itself up and down each lane.

"Mom, Principal Murphy was one of Keirnan's kidnappers."

"You've got to be kidding me?"

"No. We're trying to figure out what his connection is with all of this. School will likely be a bit solemn today. He was killed in Keirnan's rescue last night."

He heard his mom's gasp, but that white car was of more importance right now.

"Mom, I've got to get going. Are you alright? If they don't call off school today, can you get Emmy to school?"

"Yes, honey. I'm stunned. Bewildered. But, we'll be okay. I've got Emmy. You figure this all out so we can get Keirnan on the right path."

"Thanks, Mom. Love you."

He hung up and texted Auggie while he kept his eye on the white car.

*Please come to the family room asap.*

As the car continued its path and neared this side of the hospital, he could see it was that white Lincoln he'd seen earlier. So, if this man wasn't working with the ones killed last night, who in the hell was he?

The door opened and Auggie entered.

"Dane, what's up?"

Pointing to the white car he said, "That's the car. I can't see the plates on it, but I'd bet you it is. It's just perusing every car in the lot. I don't know what else he'd be doing, driving up and down each lane since that far exit." He pointed to the end of the lot. "And driving past empty parking spaces."

Auggie watched with him for a spell, then said, "Keep your eye on it, I'm going down to see if I can get a closer look."

"Be careful."

Not wanting to risk losing sight of the car, he didn't look back as Auggie left. What in the hell did this mean? Either they didn't get everyone involved or this guy was someone else stalking Keirnan. Either way, after what she'd been through, the last thing she needed was this.

The car never slowed unless someone was crossing the lane in front of it. He moved up and then turned down another lane and he saw Auggie step outside on the sidewalk. Walking toward the car, his head down a bit, it was impossible not to hold his breath. He held his phone up and his finger hovered over the "9" in case he had to dial 911. They weren't sure what they were dealing with and the last thing he wanted was for Auggie to get shot.

The car passed by where Auggie was walking, then Auggie held up his phone and snapped a few pictures. The man in the car sped off, clearly not wanting to have his picture taken.

Dane watched as the car sped down the lane to the exit driveway, never slowing down.

## 36

"Honey, do you need a drink of water?"

"No, Mom, I'm okay."

Her mom took her hand and she knew all mom wanted to do was help her, but there honestly wasn't anything she could do. Sleep was the only thing she wanted at this time, but it would be rude to tell her mom to go home so she could sleep. And, she wanted to be awake again when Dane came back in. Having him close made her feel better. Safer. Alive.

Her mom walked over to the chair that Dane had slept in last night, pulled it closer to the bed and sat down.

"I think Dane really cares for you."

She had that motherly knowing smile on her face.

"I really care for him, Mom." She stared into her mom's eyes to see where this was going. "And Emmy, too."

"It's not easy getting involved with a man who has a child. But if anyone would have a big enough heart to raise another woman's daughter, it would be you."

Hearing that made her wince. Emmy would always be

Catherine's daughter and not hers. But if things worked out with them, she'd be the best stepmom she could be. And if Catherine were looking down from heaven, she could only hope she'd be happy.

The door burst open and a breathless Lexi ran in to the side of her bed. Grabbing her hand, she blurted. "Oh, my God. I just found out you were here. How are you?"

Lexi's blue eyes met hers and held. Then her friend's eyes sparkled with moisture. "Ohh, my gawd. Honey..." Lexi's left hand came up to touch the side of her face gently. "Honey, are you okay? I mean that's stupid, of course not. Are you in pain?"

"Yes, my face hurts, my leg hurts, my wrists hurt, my ankles hurt."

That caused her friend to look down at her one visible wrist with its bruising from the tight tape binding, the abrasions from twisting and sawing to try to free herself from the chair and the swelling where she'd pulled at the tape to break it. Her right wrist was bandaged because of the cut from the chair. "Ohh." She sobbed. "Oh, sweetie." She tried keeping her tears at bay, but wasn't successful.

"Hey. I'll heal. Promise."

Lexi tried smiling. It only worked a little.

"Why are you here so early in the morning anyway?"

"I didn't sleep much last night. I was restless after I found out that you'd been kidnapped. Parents were calling me, concerned after they'd been released from the police. I called Bekah and she didn't know anything more than anyone else. So, I tossed and turned. Then this morning we got an email from school telling us that Principal Murphy was killed close to the library last night. They called school off today. I called your mom and she told me that you were here."

Lexi turned her head to Keirnan's mom, "Thank you, Elaine, if I didn't say it before."

"You're welcome, honey." Her mom's smile was genuine. She'd always liked Lexi, and the feeling was mutual.

"Anyway." Lexi turned back to her. "Was Principal Murphy trying to rescue you? Did you see him? Can you tell me what happened?"

She took a deep breath and was happy it didn't hurt. Everything else seemed to today, but that was likely because she was lying here focusing on all her aches and pains.

"Lex, Principal Murphy was one of my kidnappers. We don't know how he was involved yet, or why."

"What? That's..." They stared at each other for long moments. "Oh my God!"

"I know, I just found out myself and was still trying to process that news when you came in. I don't know what to think and to be honest, it scares the shit out of me. Who else do I know that wants to cause me harm?"

"Oh, Keirnan, this is unbelievable. I...I don't even know what to say."

She took her friend's hand in hers and squeezed. "You don't have to say anything. It just means so much to me that you're here."

Lexi inhaled deeply, swiped at the moisture under her eyes, shook her head slightly, then asked, "So was Dane here? Was he there last night? I'm sorry for all the questions, I'm just trying to get my bearings."

She reached for the remote button to lift herself up in the bed a bit more. She noted that both her mom and Lexi stood at the ready as if she were an invalid and needed constant monitoring.

"Okay, first, you two need to relax. I know I must look horrible, and to be honest, I don't feel the best this morning. Mostly still groggy and sore. But, I'm so fortunate. No vital organs were damaged and honestly you guys, I'm not fragile."

Her mom stood and took a deep breath. "I'm sorry, sweetheart, I don't mean to hover, but you need to understand that you're my baby, you always will be and I'm entitled to worry about you."

Her mom looked at Lexi then back to her. "We love you."

She let the breath in her lungs go and relaxed back into bed. She'd been tense and uncomfortable but now felt remarkably better just having let the tension go.

"I know you do and I can't tell you how much I love both of you, too. Thank you both for being here."

Lexi sniffed then smiled, "Now that we have that out of the way, where's your handsome boyfriend?"

Feeling the last of the pressure lift from her shoulders she smiled at her friend. "He's calling his mom."

The door opened and Dane and her father walked into the room. Both of them looked stone-faced and tense. Dane's back was rigid even the way he walked was stiff or determined.

"What's going on with you two?" She could feel the tension form in her body once again.

"It's nothing, honey." Her father said all too quickly.

Her eyes sought out Dane's. "Dane?"

He cleared his throat lightly then came to stand beside her bed. "It's nothing to worry about at the moment. You just need to rest and heal."

Wherever this burst of anger came from, she'd never

know but the words flew out of her mouth before her brain even registered what she wanted to say.

"Don't treat me like a child! I want to know what the hell is going on and now!"

## 37

D ane looked across Keirnan's bed at Auggie, who appeared as uncomfortable as he was. How much to tell her? They didn't have any idea what they were up against. It was impossible to guess what in the world was going on. Who would have believed Principal Murphy would do Keirnan harm?

For a second, he waited to see what Auggie would do, then decided it was time to secure his relationship with Keirnan in the same way he'd expect from her – with the truth.

"Princess, when I was talking to Mom I noticed a car in the parking lot driving up and down every lane. As it neared, I recognized it as the Lincoln that we saw outside of your house. I texted Auggie and he went down to get pictures and confirm. We have, it is the same car. What we still don't know is who's driving the car and what they want. I've called the local police department and they are now on the lookout for it."

Her hands folded over her stomach as if to stop the

quelling. Her face paled and he watched her swallow several times.

Her eyes floated up to his and held. "So, you think he was trolling the hospital parking lot looking for one of your vehicles and if he didn't see it, he may have tried coming up here to kill me?"

"We don't know. But, I've called David and between the four of us, David, Auggie..." He looked at Auggie and received a nod in reply. "Masters and I, one of us will be here around the clock to make sure you're safe."

"What happens when I leave here?"

Elaine stood next to her husband at her daughter's bedside. Lexi next to her. He stood on the opposite side of the bed but didn't feel as though it was them against him in any way. They were all unified in keeping Keirnan safe.

Elaine responded. "We'll hire security or whatever we need to do. You can come home and live with us until we all know it's safe for you."

He cleared his throat and Keirnan looked away from her mom to him. "Or you can come and live with me and Emmy. I have security and between David and myself and a couple of friends we can call in, we'll have security for you. I'll protect you as fiercely as I'll protect Emmy."

It was as if the whole room and everyone in it held their breath as they waited for her to respond. His heart hammered in his chest. He hadn't lived with a woman since Catherine and it was a big deal bringing Keirnan in with Emmy, but he wanted this. He wanted her. It felt right.

"I'd love that Dane, and I know you'll do everything you can to keep Emmy and I safe."

Whoosh, he was able to breathe again. Everyone in the room took a breath, too, and he saw Auggie and

Elaine's shoulders drop as if they were part relieved and part disappointed that she wouldn't be coming home with them.

The door to her room opened and the same nurse that had been in earlier walked in, followed by another nurse.

"Wow, full house so early this morning. Keirnan, this is Diane and she'll be your nurse during the day shift."

Diane said, "Good morning."

The two nurses then looked over Keirnan's vitals, checked her charts, then Diane came to Keirnan's bedside, which caused Auggie, Elaine and Lexi to move away, and pulled a thermometer from its electronic holder and held it in front of her. "Open please."

Auggie walked around to where Dane stood, so he backed away from Keirnan's bed and let the nurses tend to her.

"Do you have a plan?" Auggie asked.

"I haven't officially started my new job, so I'm home. David can give me a few hours a day to keep watch, remotely via security camera and we have another friend, fellow soldier, who can also give me a few hours. Between the three of us and you, we should be able to keep eyes on Keirnan 24-7. In the meantime, we need to keep investigating who is in the Lincoln, how Principal Murphy came to get hired at the school or was he paid off? If so, who paid him off? Who is Curtis Daniels and why would he want to hurt Keirnan? I have a couple of contacts who can help, who do you have?"

Auggie glanced over at his daughter, whose eyes were watching them talk, a thermometer still between her lips.

Auggie turned toward him, "I have a couple close friends who can do some research for me. I'll call them right away. And the fundraiser tomorrow?"

Dane took a deep breath, "We're going to have to cancel it."

"No. I have no intention of cancelling it. Lexi and I have worked our asses off planning it and the library, now more than ever, needs the money."

Looking into Keirnan's worried eyes his pride swelled for her. Here she was beaten and battered, a bullet hole in her leg, and she wanted to continue on as if all were okay.

Auggie stepped closer to her. "Honey, with all those people there, how on earth can we keep you safe? That is the most important thing in all of this."

"Dad, let's hire a security firm. I've got money, I'll pay for it myself. We can ask the police to have a presence. We can..." She froze. Her eyes rounded. "Did the police release the library from its custody?"

He shook his head but didn't get the chance to say any more.

Nurse Diane then interrupted. "I'll be back after breakfast to get you up and walking, Keirnan."

Keirnan mumbled, "Thank you." But turned quickly back to her father and him.

She bit the inside of her cheek, then turned to Lexi. "We need to find another place to hold the fundraiser. There must be a place in town that will allow us to continue, can you start calling places?"

"Of course, honey." Lexi responded. But she didn't sound convinced.

## 38

S itting on the edge of her bed, she let out a long breath. Her knees shook, her head felt like it was spinning in the clouds and she felt exhausted. She'd just walked down the hall, a nurse holding her with an assistance belt, as she rolled her IV cart along. To be honest, she was surprised it didn't hurt more, but the medications sure did make her feel weak and frail.

"There you go. Your sheets are all changed and now that you've had a bit of exercise, you should take a nap. I'll be back in about an hour to help you wash up and we'll see how you're feeling, but we'll need to get you up again for another jaunt down the hall."

She laid back and raised her legs up on the bed. The pull she felt from her stitches caused her to wince, but that was it.

"Okay. Thank you."

Nurse Diane moved her bedside tray close to the bed, refilled her water glass, looked at her IVs and monitors and silently slipped from the room. She'd intended to look through the notebook she had her mom bring her so she could continue to make plans for tomorrow night, but she just needed to relax her eyes for a moment. David sat outside of her door and for the moment she felt safe and able to sleep.

~

"Shh, we need to be quiet until she wakes up, Emmy."

"Okay, Daddy."

She heard the fabric of the chairs rustle a bit as Dane and Emmy sat down. She tried opening her eyes, but they were so heavy. Just a few more minutes.

"She looks like Sleeping Beauty."

Dane chuckled. "She sure does."

"Maybe you have to kiss her to wake her up. That's what the Prince does."

"That's not a bad idea."

The sound of fabric rustling, then Dane's soft lips touched hers. Opening her eyes as their lips parted, she looked up at him and smiled.

"Hi."

"It worked." Emmy clapped her hands and came to stand beside her bed.

"She wanted to see you and I wanted her to see you were fine other than a little bruised so she could sleep tonight. I hope it's okay."

"Of course." She looked down at Emmy, "Would you like to sit here on the side of the bed with me?"

Emmy's brown curls bobbed as she nodded her head. Dane lifted her up and Keirnan couldn't help it but yawn.

"I'm sorry, I just felt so tired after they had me walk down the hall."

"David said you did good."

She giggled a bit, "I suppose. It's like I'm a toddler again."

"Not quite."

"Ms. Vickers? Are you good now?"

"Yes, Emmy, I'm good. I have some bruises." She touched the side of her face gently with her left hand to show Emmy it was sore but would be fine. "And I have a cut on my leg right here." She lay her hand over the abundance of bandages on her right thigh. "But, I'm going to be just fine."

Emmy stared at her. She was a bright child; her eyes were assessing in their own way whether Keirnan was lying to her. Once she was satisfied the truth was being told, she smiled her brightest smile.

"Daddy said you're going to live with us."

She looked at Dane to see his reaction. What she saw was a beautiful smile and pride in the little girl he loved so much.

"Yes, I hope that's okay with you." She replied.

"It's good. Daddy said he'd share his room with you." Emmy giggled then leaned in as if she had a secret. "Sometimes he snores."

Dane chuckled then nudged Emmy's shoulder with his elbow. "So do you sometimes."

Emmy giggled and it was the cutest sound.

The door to her room opened and Lexi came in carrying an armload of paperwork. "Hi, everyone. Is this a good time or should I come back?"

Dane picked Emmy off the bed and said, "My mom is coming to pick up Emmy, then I'll relieve David outside, so this is good."

"Bye, Ms. Vickers. Bye, Ms. Rodgers." Emmy waved as Dane carried her to the door.

"I'll pop my head in when I get back."

She watched them leave the room, Emmy began chattering about a balloon she'd seen downstairs and Dane chuckled as he listened to her.

Lexi sighed. "He's simply dreamy."

"He is."

"Okay. Here's what I've got. I've called at least twenty places, and no one can accommodate us on such short notice. I'm not sure what to do from here. It's too cold to have the gathering at the park and I don't want to disappoint you, but I don't know what to do."

She felt crushed with disappointment. Dammit all anyway, she wanted this event to keep going so she'd feel as though life was going on.

Dane walked back into her room and his face immediately showed concern. "What's wrong?"

She opened her mouth to tell him, but closed it right away, 'cause dammit she was going to cry.

Lexi jumped in, "We can't find an alternate venue for tomorrow."

Dane walked to her bedside, opposite of Lexi and took her right hand in his.

"Honey, don't you think it would be too taxing on you so soon?"

Her lip quivered and she hated it. Tears gathered in her eyes. The sympathetic look on his face made her crumble and she let her tears flow. She hid her face in her hands and cried. In her weakened condition she was just overwhelmed by everything.

She felt her bed dip and his hand come around the back of her head and pull her into his firm chest. He said nothing, just let her cry. His steady, even breathing combined with his scent and strength was like a balm on her wounds. After a few moments, she pulled back, swiped at her tears and smiled when Lexi handed her a tissue.

Gently blowing her nose, she took a deep breath and let it out slowly.

"I simply wanted things to go on as normal, so in my head, things would start falling together as normal. I don't know how else to explain it. And, now more than ever, don't we need the library to be a safer place for everyone to go?" She sniffed a few times but his eyes were steady.

He nodded and let out a breath. "I may be able to help you. Can you give me a minute to check on something?"

## 39

He left her room and sat in the hall in the chair David had occupied. He didn't want to get her hopes up, but watching her cry tore at his heart. She'd been through so much and he understood wanting to get back to "normal". It's why he didn't leave the military when Catherine died. He needed to keep things as normal as possible for him and for Emmy.

Pulling his phone up, he dialed Zane Hanson's number. He'd called Dane for a favor once, maybe he'd be open to returning the favor.

"Dane, how are you? How is Keirnan? I heard about last night's horror from friends this morning."

He leaned back in his chair; thankful the hall was quiet.

"She's going to be alright. She's been beat up a fair amount, her beautiful face is purple and blue at the moment. And she was shot in the upper thigh. No major arteries were hit, she'll be fine soon. They've already had her up and walking this morning."

"Glad to hear it. What can I do for you?"

"Zane, Keirnan is heartbroken that the library hasn't been released by the local PD as it's still a crime scene. The fundraiser is tomorrow and she's been frantically looking for a new venue. Her friend and fellow co-hostess, Lexi, has been that is. I wondered if you knew of a place that would be able to hold around a hundred-fifty people that could accommodate the fundraiser on short notice. It's important to her. She wants things to feel normal again. And, maybe, it's a way to keep her mind off of what happened last night."

He waited during a short silence, his heart hammered in his chest, he realized just how much he didn't want to let her down.

"I can make a few calls, but what do you think of this? We could open up the factory for the event. It is not glamorous. But, I can have the guys clean and mop the floor of the lobby area. We can bring in tables and chairs and hang some decorations and do what we can to hold the event for her. It's large enough to hold that many people since the conference room walls aren't up yet and we don't have any offices built."

"Zane, that would be perfect. I know it isn't glamorous, but actually, it might just be perfect. The investors will also be able to see your new place and perhaps get a friendlier feel for it at the same time."

Zane chuckled on the other end. "If that's a yes, I'll get my guys cracking on cleaning it up. If Keirnan has decorations or anything she wants hung, just get them delivered and we'll take care of that as well. It's the least I can do. I feel so damned bad for what happened to her."

"Thank you, Zane, really. I'll give you the okay now and talk to Keirnan, I'm sure it'll be just fine with her."

"You're welcome. It's none of my business but I can't

help but wonder, who was it that kidnapped her? Do you have any information on them?"

"We know their names, though I'm not sure I can say just yet. We still don't know why or how they chose Keirnan."

"Fair enough. I'll get working over here. You have the address to reroute your guests, so unless I hear further, I'm on it."

"Thanks again, Zane, it means a lot to us."

"Yep."

The line went dead and he sat there, emotion flooding him at his good fortune. His limbs shook a little and his heart hammered in his chest. He inhaled deeply, let it out slowly and tried to get a handle on his emotions. Likely all that had transpired, and lack of sleep were finally catching up with him now. His eyes watered and he pinched the bridge of his nose as it began to tingle. Taking deep breaths and letting them out he tried counting to ten each time. He'd likely sleep like a rock tonight, but maybe in the recliner, rather than that little vinyl chair. At least he could comfortably lean back.

A nurse moved quietly past him and entered the room next door and he sat straight, stretched his back, and huffed out one more deep breath before standing to go tell Keirnan the good news. And, he silently prayed she wouldn't be pissed at him for accepting without talking to her, but they had little choice and he was trying to be expedient.

Turning and pushing her door open his heart felt lighter as he heard Lexi laughing. Looking at Keirnan he saw her smiling and looking at her friend and something told him things would be alright.

"So, I called Zane to see if he knew of any venues that

could accommodate us tomorrow and he offered the factory. The lobby area is cleared of all debris and no offices have been constructed, so it's a wide-open space and he'll have it cleaned for you. If we deliver the decorations to him, he'll have his guys decorate the room, too."

He gently sat on the edge of her bed, not wanting to jostle her leg and hoping she wasn't going to be pissed. "I told him we accept. I hope that was okay, but he's so good to offer. We don't have a lot of other options and we'll make it as nice as we can for you, I promise."

She laughed and took his right hand in both of hers. "That's simply fantastic. It won't be elegant, but then again, the library wasn't going to be, either. Thank you so much, Dane."

He leaned forward and hugged her close to him, relieved and happy he could do something to alleviate at least some of her burden.

"You two are so damned cute together it makes me jealous," Lexi quipped.

Keirnan spoke into his chest. "Shut up."

## 40

I t's not how she planned it. It's also not how she wanted it, but it was what she had to do. She'd been released from the hospital this morning. Massive bandages around her leg, at least they felt like it. Mostly because the swelling was still there. And, she had to sit in a wheelchair since too much walking made her sore and tired. The beautiful dress she'd purchased for tonight's fundraiser had to remain in her closet. To cover her legs, she opted for a long dress she'd worn a couple of times. She had bruising up and down both of them from being taped to the chair and climbing out the window, she'd abused her body escaping. But, not as badly as her captors had or would have.

But, Dane, Lexi, and her mom had all jumped right in and taken care of calling guests about the change in venue, dropping off the supplies she still had at home. The police refused to release the decorations she had at the library as everything had to stay as it was until their investigation was complete. So, Lexi went out and bought all new decorations; what they'd do with all the other ones was a puzzle to her, but they'd figure something out. Maybe wait until next year.

Dane pulled into the parking lot in front of the factory which now had a large blue and red sign across the top front of the building proudly displaying its name Astec Enterprises. That would make it easier for guests to find it for sure.

Keirnan looked over at Dane as he was watching out the windshield and up at the sign. No discernible emotion on his face, he just stared at it.

"It looks good."

He turned his face to hers, as if he'd been lost in thought and a half smile appeared on his handsome face. "Yeah, it looks good. Are you ready?"

"Yeah."

He opened his truck door and stepped down. Watching him as he walked around the truck had her worried that something was wrong. He seemed subdued and distant right now. She'd never felt that from him before. Though, admittedly, neither of them was getting much rest these days. He insisted on sleeping in the recliner in her hospital room last night, and though she heard him snore a couple of times, she knew he woke up often.

He pulled her wheelchair from the back of his truck, closed the tailgate and tonneau cover, opened the chair and wheeled it to the passenger door.

She unhooked her seat belt and tried smoothing her dress where the seat belt had creased it. The dark blue fabric wouldn't show the wrinkles too much once they were inside. Besides, there was nothing she could do about it and as her mom told her earlier, it was the last thing she should be worrying about - what she was wearing.

Lexi tried covering her bruises with makeup and it did fade them a bit, but it hurt too much to apply pressure, so once again, she'd have to deal with people's reactions. Hopefully, they'd feel so bad about how she looked that they'd open their wallets to the library fund. She'd milk that if she had to.

Dane opened her door and smiled at her. "Ready?"

"Yes, how about you?"

"You bet I'm ready."

He slid his right hand under her legs and his left hand behind her back. She wrapped her right arm around his shoulders and he easily lifted her from the truck, turned and gently sat her in the wheelchair. He graciously helped her arrange her dress, then lifted the fabric that hung behind her feet and pulled it forward and tucked it behind her legs.

"I don't want to drag this on the ground."

Closing the passenger door, pressing the key fob to lock it, he then began pushing her to the building. She laid her hand over her stomach; the butterflies became active all at once. All her hard work, and Lexi's combined with the change in venues was making her a nervous wreck. She didn't want to have gone through all of this for nothing. Not that her kidnapping had anything to do with the library, but since it had happened there, it all felt connected. And, honestly, she was rather happy that this event didn't take place there tonight, she wasn't sure she wanted to go back there just yet. She still had nightmares about her ordeal.

Dane pressed the handicap button on the wall and waited as the door whispered open. To say she was surprised when they entered the lobby area would be an understatement, she was downright shocked at the transformation of this building.

"Wow," she whispered.

Dane's left hand came up and rested on her left shoulder and he squeezed. "They did an amazing job didn't they?"

She swallowed as tears threatened to ruin the makeup Lexi managed to get on; this must have cost a fortune. It had to have taken twenty to thirty people working together to transfigure this room. This...this was everything she could have wished for tonight and then so much more.

## 41

H e was happy they'd been able to transform this large, empty room to look like something special. The floors had been scrubbed more than once. Tables and chairs had been brought in, tablecloths in deep purple now covered the tables. Lexi had found the last of the purple decorations the stores had on the shelves. There weren't enough purple decorations, so she made the decision to add silver and lighter shades of purple. Lilac she called them. Turned out purple was Keirnan's favorite color as well as her birthstone, something he took note of.

"It's just beautiful, Dane." Keirnan's voice held wonder and awe.

"They did a wonderful job with it," he replied.

"You were here helping, too."

He chuckled. "I was here setting up tables and checking the area for security. Zane's guys did all the cleaning. They hauled bucket after bucket of dirty water to the back room, refilled them with clean soapy water and then returned for more cleaning. The walls and floors were scrubbed thoroughly. The difference it's made is remarkable. Zane had a couple of electricians in this morning to hang the new light fixtures, too."

She looked up at the pretty fixtures glowing softly. "Those don't look like office fixtures."

Zane had entered the room from one of the back rooms and chuckled. "They aren't. I had them in a warehouse from a remodel my wife did a few years ago, I thought for tonight they'd do the trick."

Keirnan looked at Zane, and softly said, "Thank you so much, Mr. Hanson for all you've done. I'm beyond impressed and very thankful."

Zane stood before her, looked at her closely, then held out his hand to shake hers. As soon as she placed her hand in his, he leaned down so he was eye level with her. "I am so very sorry for what you have endured. I also know how hard you worked to make this benefit a reality; I'm simply helping out where I can. And, of course, I'll be giving you a large donation on top of this."

He winked, stood taller and nodded at them. "I've got some final touches on a machine in the back to oversee. I'll be leaving shortly to shower and change and pick up my wife, so I'll see you two later."

They watched him walk away and Keirnan sighed, "That was very nice of him. I'll send him a thank you card this week. Maybe flowers. Though that hardly seems enough."

"I'll bet it's more than he usually gets, he whispered in her ear.

He pushed her through the tables to the front table where they had the plates, plastic ware, cups and punch bowl set up. Each table had pretty sparkly centerpieces with long ribbons tied to balloons. The balloons swayed with the ribbons' movement and that of the fan softly blowing in the background.

"Well, do you approve?"

Lexi walked in with a man he assumed was her husband, John.

Keirnan giggled. "Yes, I approve."

She pushed her chair so it turned and she could watch Lexi walk toward her. Leaning down to hug Keirnan, Lexi's smile was bright.

"I think it turned out amazingly. Bekah came to help me with the decorations for a while this afternoon, but she had to leave for a meeting."

Lexi stood and looked at him. "Thanks for your help today, Dane. Keirnan, he worked so hard to help this all come together." Looking at her husband, she said, "John, this is Dane. I'm glad you two are finally meeting."

He shook John's hand and received a strong solid handshake in return. "Nice to meet you. Lexi talks about you two all the time."

"I hope it's all good. " Dane responded.

"It is for sure."

John bent and hugged Keirnan. "I'm so sorry, Keirnan for the nightmare that happened to you. But thrilled that you look ready to tackle the world or will be soon."

"Thanks, John. I feel better just being out of the hospital."

Itching to walk away for a minute and check on the security they had in place, he hoped Auggie and Elaine would get here soon. Just having back up here before the crowds begin floating in would make him feel better.

His phone rang, and he pulled it from his pocket. Glancing at the picture on his phone he stood tall, looked at Keirnan, and said, "It's mom. I need to take this, okay?"

"Of course." She smiled and he was happy to see the swelling had gone down enough that it didn't look like a grimace.

Tapping the answer icon he held his phone to his ear. "Mom, how can I help you?"

"Dane, Emmy and I are on our way. I just wondered if you needed anything?"

"I think we have everything we need. Isn't Stan coming with you?"

"No, his daughter was having a birthday party for his granddaughter tonight, so our schedules just didn't match up."

"That's too bad."

"Anyway, we'll be there in fifteen minutes."

"See you then."

Ending the call, he took a moment to walk to the opposite side of the room and check that the windows still had the wires attached at the corners. He didn't have a lot of time to install a top-notch security system, but he hoped for the time being this one would work. He'd ordered a new system for Zane, but they were waiting for it to arrive. He walked to the window alongside of the entry door. He couldn't shake the edgy feeling he had crawling up his spine. He felt 'off' somehow, but shook his head and chalked it up to lack of sleep, worry about Keirnan and Emmy and the upheaval of the past few days.

Relief fell over him when he saw Auggie and Elaine pull into the parking lot. Just behind their car was Richard Masters' truck. Now things were looking up.

He walked to the front door and waited for them to enter, shook hands and nodded at both Auggie and Masters. He gave Elaine a hug, "You look beautiful, Elaine."

She tittered, "Thank you, Dane. I'm off to see my daughter if you don't mind."

She walked away, and Auggie said, "Are we all set with security?"

"I have the system installed although it's not the permanent one for Zane. I was just checking the windows when you pulled in. As soon as David gets here, we'll have one of us covering each exit so we can watch everyone who comes and goes. The exit closest to where Keirnan is now leads out to the factory area. There is one machine back there and a couple of workers, but the door is locked from this side so no one should walk out. We'll only need to watch for anyone entering from this direction."

He turned to look at Auggie, and Masters said, "Any word on the dead guys?"

Auggie replied, "No more than we knew yesterday. I know the police are overwhelmed on this one. They haven't had a murder in this town in more than thirty years. So, I get it. But it's goddamned frustrating when as of yet we don't know who we're dealing with or why. I'm almost certain this has to do with Maklin. I just don't know who Curtis Daniels is, his connection to Principal Murphy, or why either of them was involved. I don't know who that guy in the Lincoln is, but he's staying close to Keirnan, and I can't help but think he was involved with Daniels and Murphy somehow. And we know nothing about the man Keirnan saw in the library. Dane, make sure she keeps an eye out for him."

Dane took a deep breath. "It's frustrating. Mostly, we have to get through tonight and keep Keirnan safe. Tomorrow, we need to dig in and see what we can find out on our own. Be thinking about who you know that we can tap for assistance or back up any ideas we think need investigating. I've got an uneasy feeling in my gut; something doesn't feel right."

Auggie and Masters both stared at him, waiting for more, but he didn't have more. He couldn't place what didn't feel right. He just knew, they were overlooking something.

---

## 42

Besides being sore, and feeling restricted in this wheelchair, tonight was coming together like a dream. Not for one minute did she think it had been easy on Dane, Lexi and her parents. She was so blessed to have them in her life. Oh, she was so enamored with Dane. With his strength. His dedication. His love for and devotion to Emmy and his mom. He was a truly decent man and a wonderful father. And, yes, she'd fallen in love with him. But, there was something not right about him tonight. Distracted. Distant. It was beginning to wear on her nerves. Maybe she was getting way ahead of him in terms of where they were in their relationship. She watched him talking to her dad, Rich Masters and David. His eyes roamed around the room often, and he always seemed to look her way, but he didn't smile. He'd glance at her then continue on with his perusal of the room, or his conversation.

She rotated her head and pulled her shoulders back to relieve the knots growing in her neck. Too much had gone on in the past few days and her body was telling her to slow down. She secretly thought tonight should have been cancelled. Everyone wanted her to cancel the fundraiser; but she just couldn't do it. Her mother called her stubborn, and, in many ways, she was. But so was her mom. This fundraiser was crucial to the repair of the library and her *Read with Your Littles* program. More importantly, because this event reminded her of her horrible ordeal, she simply had to get past it so she could focus on healing and her relationship with Dane and Emmy.

Dane walked her way and her heart began beating faster. She sat straighter in her chair and turned it so she was facing him.

He knelt down in front of her and smiled, though it didn't reach his eyes, "So, are you ready to get into position? We have the registration table set up at the front door. You'll be there to greet everyone after they've been searched for weapons. We have wands and our security detail has been briefed and are in place at the entry way. The caterers have been checked and are bringing in the food through the East side door; Masters is checking the food containers and keeping track of them. The DJ is here and checked, but he'd like to speak with you about the schedule of events."

"Okay."

He pushed her toward the corner of the room where the DJ was finishing his setup. He stopped when he saw her coming toward him and froze.

"What happen..."

She smiled and raised her hand to stop him. "I had a bit of an incident a couple of days ago. That's why all the security."

"Oh, no, that was you? I saw it on the news and

wondered what had transpired, but I've been off social media for a while and hadn't heard anything further. Today Lexi simply called to tell me to come here instead of the library, but I didn't ask her anything about what happened at the library. I'm so sorry."

"Thank you, Barry. I'm just trying to move on now." She glanced around the room and was so happy.

Pulling a sheet of paper from her purse, she opened it to show Barry the schedule of events for tonight. "Here's a copy of the schedule. If you have any questions, please ask me. Otherwise, I think you'll see it's rather straight forward. We'll have soft music while the guests are arriving. I'll do some announcements at 6:00 inviting the guests to enjoy the buffet and drinks. Soft music during the meal, then we'll begin to accept donations at which time the music tempo should increase, and you can start your performance and the auction to get folks giving."

"I'm ready."

"Wonderful." She looked up at Dane who was watching the people coming in the door.

"Hey, is everything alright?"

His head shook once as if he'd been distracted by something and turned to her, "Yes, sorry." He pushed her away from Barry a few feet, then stopped, walked around in front of her and knelt down. His voice was soft when he spoke.

"Princess, this event can go on without you tonight. I just hate having you here when we don't know who is after you or what we're up against. I just can't relax while there are so many unknown people and variables tonight.

She touched his face with the backs of her fingers, brushing them down his cheek, then she cupped his face with both of her hands.

"Dane, look at all the security. You have done a fantastic job of making sure I'm protected."

"We can't be sure of everything, Keirnan."

He held both of her hands in both of his and squeezed. "I don't want to lose you. I don't want anything to happen to you."

His eyes glistened with moisture and he blinked rapidly to clear them.

Her heart grew to double its size. "Dane, I love you."

She hadn't intended on saying it, not here or this minute, but she saw the emotion in his eyes. She felt his strength and fear. And, dammit, it felt right.

He leaned up and kissed her lips softly. His hands framed her face and held her in place, and she felt as if they were the only ones in the room. He pulled away just an inch.

"I love you, Keirnan Vickers."

And suddenly, her life felt full, fantastic and fear slipped away from her. He'd protect her no matter what, and so would her father. They'd generate a large amount of money tonight and rebuild what needed to be built at the library. Actually, she felt as if she could do anything she wanted to do now.

Giggling she kissed his lips again. "Wow, that felt and sounded simply wonderful."

For the first time tonight, he smiled and it reached his eyes.

"Dane, your mom and daughter are here," Lexi said. The smile on her face was brilliant. Lexi winked then walked over to check on the food table.

Dane stood and walked behind her chair to push her toward the doorway. Estella and Emmy made their way toward them, both with huge smiles on their faces.

"You both look gorgeous," she said as they neared.

Emmy stopped and spun around. "Do you like my new dress? Gram and me went shopping today."

Dane gently corrected her, "Gram and I, honey."

Emmy stopped, looked up at Dane and giggled. "Oops, I forgot."

"Dane." She looked up to see Rich calling to Dane.

He leaned down to whisper in her ear. "Sit tight, I'll come and get you when it's time for you to greet your guests."

## 43

The grim look on Masters' face didn't bode well. He watched his eyes the few steps it took him to reach Masters.

"We found a window pried open in the back."

"Fuck." He muttered but Masters heard him.

"Roger that." Masters looked around just as a group of people came through the door. He didn't recognize any of them and looked over to see Keirnan smiling and waving to two of the women in the group. She leaned forward and said something to his mom and Emmy then began to roll herself toward him. She halted and looked at him, remembering he'd asked her to stay put.

He nodded and decided someone would have to be next to her the whole time. At least until he could go and check things out.

"Where's Auggie?"

"Checking out the window."

"Okay." Keirnan was nearly to him, but the two women walked around him to greet her and for the time being, she was safe. Lexi was at the registration table and giving donors a list of auction items and pointing to the tables set up with the articles on display. Elaine was talking with some people she knew and a few other people were milling about, looking at the items to bid on.

That left his mom and Emmy, who were looking at the table decorations. He hated to do it, but he needed someone he could trust and he trusted no one more than his mom. After all, he trusted her with his daughter on a daily basis.

Waving to his mom, she took Emmy's hand and moved toward him through the tables.

"Daddy, the tables are so pretty."

He smiled at his sweet little girl. She was always so damned happy. "They are, aren't they, Princess?"

Her beautiful head bobbed and he saw Keirnan look over at them and smile. She'd likely hearing him call Emmy Princess.

"Mom, I have to go in the back and check something and I need to make sure Keirnan has someone with her at all times. I hate to ask you, but I won't be long, do you mind staying close to her for a few minutes?"

"Of course not, Dane. We'll be fine."

"Okay. Stay in this room, please."

"Is everything okay?"

"I hope so, but I have to check something out."

He kissed his mom's cheek, bent down to Emmy, and said, "You stay here with Gram and Keirnan. I'll be right back."

Emmy nodded her head and he nodded to his mom, then took off outside to find Auggie.

The cooler spring air helped to refresh him as he walked around the building. Auggie was looking at a window, taking pictures of the area and actually dusting for fingerprints. The man had a fingerprint kit.

"Now I feel a little out-tooled. You have your own fingerprint kit?"

"I bought it this morning. The police can't work fast enough for me and I'll do anything I can to find out who is behind this."

Impressive. "What do you have so far?"

"Whoever did this, came across the grass here." He walked away a few steps and pointed to the grass. "They or he have large feet by the size of the prints." He positioned his foot next to one of the prints to emphasize his theory.

"I'm a size 11, so I'm guessing this as a size 13 or so."

Dane looked at the two and nodded his head. "I'd say you're about right."

Auggie nodded.

"It looks like they or he got the window completely open. So, they're either already inside or are planning on coming in later. Do you have any more friends you can call to come in and help us watch things?"

Pulling out his phone he began scrolling through his contacts. "I have a couple. Not sure if they're available, but I'll ask."

The phone rang twice as he called Manny Espinosa, also known as Riptide.

"Dane, what the fuck are you up to?"

If the situation weren't so grim he'd laugh. "Manny, I need some help. Quickly. In a nutshell, my girlfriend was kidnapped, beaten and shot a few days ago and we're now at a fundraiser she insisted on holding. I'm afraid whoever orchestrated the kidnapping is here. I need some muscle onsite as well as eyes and ears."

"I'm on it. Tell me where to be."

"I'll text you the address. Any chance you can call Maddog and get him to come with you?"

"On that, too. In a few."

The line went dead and he texted the address and sent up a quick silent prayer thanking God for such great friends.

"Okay, I've got two more coming in."

"Roger. You want inside or outside?"

"I'd like to keep my eyes on Keirnan if you don't mind." His stomach was rolling. He'd been outside too long and the parking lot was filling up.

"Stay in touch. When your guys get here, tell them to come out to see me and I'll fill them in without all the ears."

"Roger."

He walked around the building to the front door, scanning the parking lot as he did. That's when his heart nearly pounded through his chest.

He took off at a run to get inside to Keirnan. Hopefully he wasn't too late.

## 44

Entering the building, he was stuck behind a large group coming into the fundraiser. Not wanting to create panic he tried successfully escaping through the crowd. Finally making his way inside, he turned right to get to the spot where Keirnan would be greeting her guests. She wasn't there, neither was his mom or Emmy.

Lexi was still at the table handling the registration. The room had filled considerably and looking over the heads in the room proved to be impossible. The DJ was in place and soft music pervaded the room; the makeshift bar had a line in front of it with eager attendees. The auction tables were lined with people, no Keirnan, Emmy or his mom.

Lexi looked up at him, "Dane, Keirnan, Emmy and your mom are in the women's room. Emmy couldn't wait."

She raised her shoulder and smiled.

He walked to the short hall where both bathrooms were situated. He listened at the women's bathroom door; he didn't hear anything so he knocked.

The door opened a crack, and his mom peered out.

"Dane, honey, what's wrong?"

"I couldn't find you."

His heart hammered in his chest and he struggled to control his breathing. His fingers shook slightly.

"Oh, we're all in here, Emmy couldn't wait and Keirnan took the time to use the facilities, too. We'll be out in a minute, honey. Why don't you wait for us by the DJ?"

She closed the door and his jaw tightened. Looking across the room at the DJ, what he saw was a man with long, brown hair watching him with the most eerie stare. He stepped to the entry way and spoke to David.

"Something's not right in there. The white Lincoln is outside and I'm beginning to worry that we need all hands-on deck inside. I'm going out to bring Auggie inside. Please step inside and watch from a close distance the man standing by the DJ with the long, brown hair. Keirnan, my mom, and Emmy are supposed to meet me there when they leave the women's room. Grab Masters. I've got Maddog and Riptide on their way. I'll send them in when as soon as I can.

"Roger." David walked into the room without another word.

Stepping outside, he took in a deep breath of air then jogged around the building to where he'd left Auggie.

What he found made his blood run cold. Auggie laid crumpled on the ground, a large gash in the back of his head, blood oozing from it. The window was now open but, looking through the window into the well-lit room, he couldn't see anyone. Running back to the front of the building, he entered and not too gently pushed people out of the way. David stood in front of the man by the DJ talking to him. The conversation looked heated. He ran to the women's bathroom and shoved open the door, only to see Keirnan standing against the wall with her hands behind her back. His mother lying on the floor with a gash in the back of her head.

A brunette woman of medium height pivoted to him and turned the gun she had been pointing at Keirnan on him. Without a second's hesitation, he pulled his weapon and fired. He heard Emmy's little voice scream in terror and saw her little arms wrap around Keirnan's legs. Keirnan was standing in front of Emmy to protect her and block her view.

The bathroom door burst open and Riptide and Maddog rushed in, guns drawn.

"Auggie needs assistance outside and the man with long, brown hair by Ferrance I suspect is an accomplice. He's likely armed."

They turned and ran out of the bathroom. Dane stepped close to the woman and kicked her gun away from her. He checked for a pulse, couldn't find one, and looked up at Keirnan, who'd picked Emmy up and was keeping her face averted and trying to console her while leaning against the wall for support. Glancing around the room, he saw her wheelchair shoved into one of the stalls. He skirted the woman lying on the floor, dead eyes staring at the wall. That's when he realized who she was and his heart raced out of control while his brain reeled in disbelief.

Walking to Keirnan and Emmy, he wrapped his arms around both of them and held them close, Emmy still screaming albeit less loudly. Keirnan sobbed into the crook of his shoulder and Emmy's little arms clung to Keirnan's neck. He could feel her shaking and Emmy heaving out big breaths but he just held them close. There'd be time for talking later.

Commotion could be heard outside and he knew the fundraiser was coming to an abrupt end. She'd worked so hard for this, but it wasn't meant to be. Not this time anyway.

Letting go of Keirnan and Emmy, he turned and checked on his mom, who'd begun to stir. Trying to sit up, she held the back of her head with one hand while holding herself up with the other hand. Her eyes glanced across the floor at Bekah lying on the ground and she bit the inside of her cheek.

"Bitch hit me on the back of the head with something."

"Yeah. Words." He nodded his head to Emmy and his mom mouthed. "Sorry."

Helping his mom to her feet, he asked, "Are you okay to stand?"

"Yes. I don't want to be on the floor by her."

He understood. She held herself up using the door of one of the stalls and he went back to Emmy and Keirnan.

Emmy had calmed a bit and looked up at him, held her arms out to be hugged and he scooped his little girl up in his arms and held her tight. Catherine was looking down on her tonight.

After a few moments, he whispered. "Are you alright?"

Both of them nodded their heads.

"Ms. Vickers said bad words to Ms. Bekah."

He tried hiding his smile as he looked at Keirnan, but it was just the levity he needed right then. Keirnan blushed and shrugged.

"Was it because Ms. Vicker's was scared?"

"Yeah. She tected me."

"Protected."

"Yeah."

Keirnan giggled and rubbed Emmy's back. Then using her arms, pushed herself off the wall. Looking down at Bekah's body, Keirnan swallowed but didn't flinch. Hanging on to the wall, she began making her way to her wheelchair.

"I can get it, Princess."

Shaking her head, no, then nodding toward Bekah's body, he began backing away from Bekah, trying to obstruct Emmy's eyes from her.

"Hey, Emmy, let's help Keirnan get her wheelchair, okay."

Emmy turned her head toward the wheelchair and nodded.

Keirnan slowly made progress, keeping her face neutral and not showing signs of pain, but he saw her hands trembling and knew her legs likely were as well.

He walked to the stall hiding her chair and pulled it out with one hand. Emmy turned her head in the direction of Bekah, and he said, "Hey, can you reach down and help me out?"

Emmy stopped and looked shocked into his eyes for a moment, then twisted in his arms and reached toward the wheelchair and he turned it toward Keirnan.

She sat with a thud, letting out a shaky breath, then took a deeper shaky breath and turned her wheelchair to the door, keeping her eyes turned away from Bekah. Dane placed Emmy on Keirnan's lap, on her good leg. She'd been betrayed twice in just three days and this would likely keep her from trusting in the future. He was grateful she already knew him, or it would be tough getting through that wall she'd likely just built.

He walked ahead of them to the door, opened it up

and his mom took hold of the wheelchair and he let them move out before him, reminding them quickly, "Just stay in the hall here until we know the stampede to get out is over."

"Okay." Keirnan replied. And two more steps and he allowed the bathroom door to close behind him.

"I've got to find out how Auggie is."

"What happened to my dad?"

## 45

"Then what happened?"

The police detective that questioned her was thorough, she'd give him that. She repeated, for the third time, the events of the evening.

"Emmy had to use the bathroom. Estella was asked by Dane to stay with me, so she asked me to come with them, so she wouldn't go back on her word. It was bad timing, because most of the guests were just beginning to come in, but she was worried that Dane would be mad if she left me, so we all went together. A while later Dane knocked on the door and Estella told him we'd be right out and to meet us by the DJ. He left and then the door opened again shortly thereafter; Estella thought it was Dane and rolled her eyes, but Bekah came in and hit her on the head with the butt of her gun. Estella dropped to the floor and Emmy began crying. Bekah yelled at her and told her to shut the fuck up or she'd be next and it made Emmy cry even harder.

I stood up and grabbed Emmy's hand, moving her back to the wall behind me. Bekah told me she was taking me with her because her dad wasn't finished with me yet. She said she wanted my dad, for the rest of his life, to know how they'd tortured me before they killed me to pay for what he'd done to her sister."

She took a deep breath and let it out slowly. Just thinking of how things could have turned out so differently was sobering.

"Then what happened?"

She rubbed her temples with shaking fingers before answering. "Dane came in, Bekah turned to shoot him, and he shot her first."

"How do you know Bekah would have shot him?"

"She pointed a gun at him."

"She was pointing a gun at you, too."

She nodded. She was tired and she didn't want to have to keep going over this.

"They had other plans for me that didn't include killing me. Just yet, I guess, as I just told you."

She cleared her throat and fidgeted in her chair. Rubbing her forehead with the pads of her fingers, she wondered where Dane, Emmy and Estella were.

"How's my dad, and how is Estella? Can you tell me that?" They'd taken her to a back room in Zane's factory while they questioned her.

"My information tells me they both have a headache. They've been given something for the pain, had their heads bandaged and are resting comfortably in the next room."

"When can I see them?"

The officer closed his tablet, stood, and said, "I can take you to them now. I think I've gotten everything I need here."

She exhaled. "Thank you so much."

He opened the door and she maneuvered the chair through it, then waited to see which way he would turn. Instead, he surprised her by grabbing the handles and wheeling her to the left.

He reached forward and opened the door to the room where the benefit had been. There were two gurneys the EMTs must have brought in, Estella on one with a sleeping Emmy lying in her arms and her father on the other. Her mom sat in a chair in the corner closest to her dad, looking at her phone. She stood up as the officer rolled her in.

Coming to hug her, her mom whispered in her ear.

"I was so worried about you. How are you, honey?"

"I'm fine, Mom. Super tired though."

"How's your leg? Your bandages likely need changing."

"The EMTs did that for me. I'm just sore."

Her mom stooped further and hugged her again. She wrapped her arms around her mom's shoulders and the tears flowed. Mom knelt down on the floor, but didn't lose the hug, and was able to hug her closer. She cried into her mom's shoulders, and loved the feel of being wrapped in her mom's arms.

Mom let her cry herself out and she needed it. It had been a horrible week. Besides being kidnapped and assaulted, the betrayals of two people she knew, simply shook her to her core. She kept feeling like everyone would do the same. As she settled, she sat back and swiped at her tears. Her mom stood and grabbed a napkin that had been left on a table in the corner and brought it to her, then sat in the chair next to her and quietly waited.

After cleaning herself up, she looked over at her dad, Estella and Emmy and quietly asked her mom, "How are they?"

Her mom looked over at them, a sad but soft smile on her face, clearly her emotions were mixed. "They'll have headaches, but no lasting effects from what we can tell. EMTs looked them over and bandaged them up. Of course, they both declined hospital stays. Emmy is fine, scared of course, but as long as someone is hugging her, she settles down.

Emmy yawned and rubbed her eyes. Estella instinctively tightened her arms around her. Estella's eyes opened and immediately found her.

She struggled to sit, which woke Emmy up.

Emmy climbed off the cot and looked at her. She opened her arms to the sweet little girl and her heart pumped faster when she hesitated, that didn't last long, and Emmy came to her. She scooted between the footrests in the wheelchair and Keirnan was able to hug her close. Lifting her up to sit on her good leg, she felt at peace holding this precious little girl. Emmy lay her head on Keirnan's chest and Keirnan wrapped her arms around her tightly, resting her cheek on the top of Emmy's head. They sat quietly for a while, just letting their hearts heal together, enjoying a few quiet and peaceful moments. This was one of those times where it was a comforting quiet.

Her dad opened his eyes and watched her hug Emmy. After a few moments, he sat up slowly, his eyes landing on each person in the room.

Quietly he asked, "Any news on Dane, Masters or Ferrance?"

She shook her head slowly and her mom got up and walked to her dad's cot, looked at the bandage at the back of his head, checked him for fever, then lay her head on his shoulder and wrapped her arms around his waist.

Her eyes sought Estella's. "How are you?"

She smiled and touched the back of her head. "I'll be fine. Dane tells me all the time I'm hardheaded, I guess it came in handy this time."

She giggled because it seemed so funny at this moment in time.

Emmy sat up on her lap and knocked on her own head with her little knuckles. "My head is hard, too."

Estella smiled at her granddaughter and Keirnan laughed. It felt so good to laugh just a little. Life had been far too somber recently.

The door to their room opened and Dane walked in.

## 46

Sitting next to his mom, Emmy on his lap, Keirnan's hand in his, his heart felt whole again. They made it through this horrific ordeal, but there was still an unrest in his soul. A burning need that was churning and he thought he knew what it was but needed to talk it out, without Emmy around.

"We're free to go home," he told them.

He winked at Keirnan, and whispered close to her ear. "If mom isn't comfortable alone, do you mind if she comes home with us?"

"Of course not." She didn't even need to think about it, it was a given.

"Mom, if you want to come home with us, we have room."

"Dane and Keirnan, thank you for the offer, but I want my own bed, in my own house. I'll be fine and sleep better if I'm comfortable."

"What about your injury, shouldn't you be with someone in case you need help?" Keirnan asked her.

"I promise to keep my phone close and I'll call if I need help. You're close. I have neighbors and I'll be fine."

Emmy took that opportunity to pipe up. "Gram has a hard head."

Everyone chuckled at his little girl's comment. She was priceless.

Auggie stood, "Dane, what about the others?"

"They've just left and said they'll touch base tomorrow. Maklin is in jail."

Auggie nodded, his eyes darted to Keirnan's then back to his.

His voice cracked. "I'm so sorry, honey." Taking a deep breath to get his emotions under control, Elaine rubbed his back and held his left hand in her right one.

"Daddy, don't...we can talk about it another time." Her eyes darted to Emmy and Auggie nodded.

Taking in a deep breath, Dane set Emmy on her feet and stood. His mom stood, reached out to steady herself by holding on to his arm, and he looked into her eyes.

"I'll drive you home. We can come and get your car tomorrow. No arguments."

Estella nodded, then he looked down at Keirnan. "Let me get them in the truck and I'll come back and get you."

"I'll take Keirnan to the truck, Dane," Auggie said as he stepped toward them.

Auggie grabbed hold of the handles on the back of her wheelchair and began pushing her toward the door. He followed with his mom and Emmy in tow. Elaine moved ahead of them and opened the door in the entry-way. He walked his mom to the back-driver's side door and opened it for her, steadying her as she stepped up into his truck. Once she was sitting, he closed the door and walked Emmy around to the passenger side of the truck. Opening the door, he glanced over and saw his mom had buckled her seat belt. Lifting Emmy up to her car seat, he helped her buckle in, then turned, closed the door and reached forward for Auggie's hand to shake.

"I'd like to speak with you tomorrow if you're up to it."

Elaine interrupted, "Why don't you all come over for lunch, I'll make some comfort food and we'll be able to sit and visit and regroup."

"Perfect."

He glanced down at Keirnan. "Is that good with you, Princess?"

When she smiled his heart felt whole. He hadn't seen that in a while and it was weird how it weighed on him.

"That sounds perfect. Not sure how much cooking I'll be able to do for a while."

Elaine leaned down and kissed Keirnan on the cheek. "Don't worry about that, I'll fix you up some meals and bring them over. See you tomorrow. I love you."

"I love you, too, Mom."

Elaine stood, nodded to him and said, "Bring your mom, too."

Without waiting for an answer she turned and walked to their car.

Auggie chuckled. "She's in mamma bear mode, so it's best to just listen to her and not argue."

He leaned down and kissed Keirnan. "I love you, girl. See you tomorrow."

Nodding once he turned and followed Elaine.

Dane leaned down and whispered, "Ready?"

"Yeah."

Keirnan leaned down and folded up her footrests, then took his hand and lifted herself to stand. Once she was steady, he pushed the chair away, kissed her lips softly and rested his forehead to hers.

"All I want right now is to lie with you in bed and hold you in my arms. You'll never know how scared I was to see a gun pointed at you. I'll never have the words. I never want to see that again."

"You'll never know how happy I was to see you walk in that door. And, being wrapped up in your arms sounds like a piece of heaven right now."

He kissed her again. "We better get going then."

He leaned down and picked her up, set her in the truck and waited as she situated herself.

Closing her door, he walked around the truck and saw Auggie and Elaine watching them. He smiled and nodded, then hopped up into his truck eager to get home.

An hour later, his mom was home, Emmy was tucked into her bed and Keirnan was lying in his bed, now their bed, for the time being anyway, but he had a pretty good sense where this relationship was going. The lights were turned off, the doors were locked, he checked the security system and walked toward the bedroom.

Peeling his clothes off, he climbed into bed, happy that they'd finally made it home and to this point. Keirnan scooted toward him and his arms eagerly pulled her closer. Her right leg still bandaged, was on his side, so he kissed her lips, then urged her to her left side, where he could spoon with her while they both fell asleep.

*Catherine walked into the room, and slowly made her way to the bed. His heart hammered in his chest as she looked down at Keirnan lying in his arms, then looked into his eyes. He hadn't seen her in such a long time and he wasn't sure what to do. He'd loved her, still had love for her in his heart, but he loved Keirnan. Catherine then looked down at Keirnan peace-fully sleeping then looked at him again and smiled. She nodded slowly, then lifted her hand to her lips, kissed her fingers and blew the kiss to him. Slowly she turned and walked out the door.*

Dane's eyes flew open. He glanced at the clock on the bedside table on Keirnan's side the bed. Three o'clock in the morning. He was covered in a fine sheen of sweat, his heart raced and his mind felt foggy. He looked at the bedroom door, and it was closed. Closing his eyes, he recalled what he'd just seen and in his heart he knew Catherine had just given him her blessing.

## 47

Giggling in the distance woke her up. She laid there for a minute more and heard giggling again and she smiled. What a nice way to wake up. Taking a deep breath, she reached down and touched the bandages on her leg, checking for warmth and tenderness. The warmth wasn't any more than body temperature, the tenderness, of course, was still there, but didn't seem as bad as yesterday.

Glancing at the clock next to her, she saw it was 8:30. The sunlight shone through the window across the room, filtering through the crack alongside the pulled blinds. A new day.

Sitting up she twisted to hang her legs off the side of the bed and was pleased that didn't hurt as badly as it had yesterday.

Allowing herself to slide off the bed, landing on her good foot, she waited as she balanced herself, then nodded and smiled. Using the bed for support, she walked to the edge of the bed and smiled when she saw Dane had set out a pair of sweatpants and a t-shirt for her to wear.

Today, she'd have to go to her house and get some clothes. And they'd have to talk about how long she'd be at his house and where they were going from here. She knew what she wanted, but she wasn't sure what Dane wanted. As she slipped his t-shirt over her head, she remembered the dream she had last night. A beautiful blond woman came into the bedroom and smiled down at her, blew Dane a kiss and left.

"Catherine." She whispered.

Sitting on the edge of the bed, she stared off into space remembering the peaceful expression on her face. And, strangely, after all she'd been through, she remembered not being afraid of her.

Bending to slip her injured leg into the sweatpants she gently slid them up her leg and over the bandages on her thigh. Being a woman and all, she couldn't help but wonder how much of a scar she'd have, then silently scolded herself for not being more grateful it wasn't a fatal shot. She could cover a scar.

Slipping her good leg into Dane's sweatpants, she stood and pulled them up, grateful they had a tie at the waist. Emmy's giggling could be heard and she couldn't wait to go and see what she was giggling at.

Deciding to try and make it down the hall without her chair, she went from the bed, to supporting herself on the dresser, then on the wall. She opened the door and limped into the hallway, staying close to the wall for support. Each step felt like a pinch in her thigh, but it was bearable. She probably couldn't walk very far like this, but she could manage this.

"Daddy, that's funny," Emmy giggled again.

The aroma of bacon cooking reached her nose and after she passed Emmy's room and the bathroom, she entered the kitchen. There stood Dane at the counter, a griddle in front of him and he was squirting pancake batter onto the griddle from a squirt bottle, making happy faces. Emmy had a chair pulled up to the counter watching him.

She stood a moment, watching him play with his daughter, his smile was beautiful. Actually the whole man was beautiful. He had such a strong heart. He had honor, and loyalty beyond any she'd ever known and she felt absolutely lucky to be with him. With them.

He looked up and his eyes landed on hers and held for a long time. His smile was broad and bright. Then his eyes rounded and he ran around the counter.

"I brought your chair out here last night so you wouldn't trip on it if you got up. Let me grab it."

"No, it's okay. I'll just sit here at the table if you don't mind. I'm feeling a bit better today."

He walked to her then, wrapped his arms around her and held her close. He smelled fantastic. He felt fantastic. She wrapped her arms around his waist and enjoyed the feel of him against her.

"You guys stop that." Emmy giggled.

He pulled back, looked into her eyes, kissed her lips softly and much too briefly, then said, "Good morning."

"Good morning." She limped to the table and sat down while Dane ran back to the griddle to flip his pancake. "Morning, Emmy."

"Morning, Ms. Vickers."

Her eyes floated to Dane's and she scrunched her nose. He nodded to her knowing what she meant.

"Emmy, honey. You can call me Keirnan when we're at home."

Emmy giggled, "That seems funny to me."

"I suppose it does. You can pick what you want to call me."

"Okay I'll think about it."

She laughed and Dane joined in. "Fair enough."

Dane took the pancakes off the griddle and brought them to the table.

"Emmy, can you bring the forks to the table?"

"Sure." She hopped down from her chair and walked around the counter where Dane handed her three forks.

He smiled at Emmy as she walked to the table, then looked up at her and winked.

Bringing the plates and pancakes to the table, he efficiently turned and pulled the bacon from the microwave and set it on the table.

"Would you like coffee?"

"Oh, yes, please."

He poured them each a cup, poured Emmy a glass of milk in a cup with a straw, and brought them all to the table.

"We need to say grace before we eat," he said; and held his hands out to each of them. She reached across the table to hold Emmy's hand and they bowed their heads as Dane led them in prayer. Life was going to be alright.

## 48

L unch was an amazing roast beef, potatoes and carrots. His belly was stuffed, his heart was over-flowing, his life was full, except for one thing.

"Auggie, can I have a private word?"

Auggie nodded and stood as Elaine, Keirnan and his mom began clearing the table. Keirnan insisted on doing something, though she was slower, but it made her feel good to help. He looked up at her as she took his plate.

"Can you watch Emmy? I need to talk to your dad for a minute."

"Of course." She smiled and bent to kiss his lips, which still gave him a thrill.

He stood and followed Auggie to his office where they closed the door. He sat in a tall backed leather chair as Auggie sat behind his desk. It was a large mahogany desk, which suited this man.

"What's on your mind, Dane?"

He leaned forward and put his elbows on his knees.

"I can't get past this black area between the police and the military and where people, like us during this ordeal, fall through the cracks. The cops have to follow so many rules and regulations. There's a real need for an organization who can go in, get shit done and bug out."

Auggie leaned forward and pierced him with his eyes. Blue as an ocean usually, they now took on a dark tone to them, like cold water.

"And."

"I got a job with Zane, as you know. I can do that job and it'll be fine. But, what I fear is that I'll struggle to feel relevant. I want to start a group like that. Trouble is, I'm not sure I have the contacts I need. I believe the government would seek out and hire a group like this to go in and do the things they can't do. We would then fill in the gap between the military and police agencies. Less or no rules. Covert. Your PsyOps training, contacts and experience, my experience in special forces and anyone else we recruit, would be topnotch and fill that void."

Auggie sat back in his chair and stared at him. It seemed like an hour, no words spoken, did he even blink?

Then he finally responded. "I'll be honest here, Dane, I thought you were going to ask for my daughter's hand in marriage."

Dane smiled, "That was next, Auggie."

"Fair enough. I've been thinking the same thing. I was about to go out of my mind while Keirnan was kidnapped. Waiting and waiting and waiting while they had to follow all of their protocols. It just about sent me out of my mind."

Leaning forward again, he said, "And, we're on the same page. I've made those contacts. I have a new guy working with me. He's with the State Department. I can't disclose his name but I've been talking with him about all of this. He's in. He can float us the work. But, the caveat is, if we get caught, the State Department doesn't know us, the military doesn't know us. He can help a bit with some police agency shielding, but we'd be largely on our own."

Dane smiled. Yes! That's what he wanted. He knew they could do that. He sat staring straight ahead, at nothing in particular. It sounded perfect.

Auggie cleared his throat and Dane looked at him. "And the answer is yes."

His smile grew as large as the meaning dawned on him. He nodded and stood.

"Next steps?"

"You need to get out of that job. Marry my daughter while I set up this group. What do you think of the name GHOST? Government Hidden Ops Specialty Team?"

"I think it's perfect. What do you think of a wedding next month?"

"I think it's perfect. Also, I've mentioned this to Masters as well, you good with him?"

"Absolutely. Ferrance?"

"Yep."

"Great, I just have to get the bride to agree." He nodded at his future father-in-law which made him laugh.

"By the looks of things, I think she'll be agreeable."

Dane nodded. "Any news on Maklin and Murphy and how they were tied together with Daniels?"

"Daniels is Maklin's son. Bekah was Maklin's daughter. She was much younger and likely born after his older daughter was killed in the explosion. As to Murphy, he had some kiddie porn on his computers at home and at school and Maklin used that against him to get him to do his bidding. The whole mess was orchestrated around revenge against me."

Dane shook his head. "You could never have guessed

that. Never have known. I presume it was Maklin in the white Lincoln?"

Auggie simply nodded, no other words were needed.

"And the man Keirnan saw in the library?"

"Daniels."

Dane huffed out a breath and stood. He left the room and Auggie followed behind him. He and Keirnan needed to have a long and serious conversation and then he needed to contact Zane. Then David.

It might prove to be a long night.

## 49

Emmy was settled into bed at 7:00 sharp. She'd begun to get crabby and it had been a long couple of days. Bedtime was calling.

He made some popcorn and brought it and two glasses of wine into the living room to sit and have a talk with Keirnan. Two talks actually, but who was counting?

He settled next to her on the sofa, turned off the television, and kissed her lips.

"I'd like to have a talk with you. It's important."

"Okay. I think it's time to have that talk."

He took her hand in his, and looked into her eyes.

"Keirnan, the second I laid eyes on you, I knew my life was about to change. You've had some tough times recently and, if this is too soon, we can table this, but I love you."

She smiled and it was as if a light turned on in the room.

"I love you, too."

"Will you marry me?"

Her eyes widened. "Really?"

He chuckled and shook his head. "Yes, really. Honestly, I wouldn't have brought you into my home with my daughter, if I didn't already know I wanted to spend my life with you. What's the saying? 'When you know, you know.'"

"To be honest, I wouldn't have agreed to come here if I didn't know. I just wasn't sure you were there yet."

"I'm there. With all that has transpired in the past few days, what I know is I want you in our lives. I need you with me because I feel whole with you. I can't imagine a better mother for Emmy. And that's the God's honest truth."

Her eyes filled with tears. "I saw her last night. Catherine. She came into the bedroom and smiled at me. I thought I was dreaming. Maybe I was, but she was peaceful. And beautiful. And, I think she likes me."

Looking at her through the tears that filled his eyes, he said, "I saw her, too. She smiled at us lying together, blew me a kiss and left. I think she was giving me her blessing."

Keirnan swiped at a tear that floated down her cheek. "That's what I felt, too."

"Will you be my wife and Emmy's mom?"

Her right hand covered her lips. Tears spilled down her cheeks, but she nodded her head.

"Yes," she managed to say before covering her mouth again.

"I haven't had the chance to buy a ring, but I thought we all could go ring shopping tomorrow."

Her arms wrapped around his neck as she lunged forward, careful not to bump her leg. He gently pulled her forward to sit on his lap. Wrapping his arms around her he pulled her as close as he could and reveled in how she felt in his arms and how fantastic life was at this very moment. They sat like that for a long time, until she stopped crying and until his heartbeat slowed to its normal tempo.

"I have to tell you more, Princess."

She pulled back to look at him.

"Your dad and I are going to start a secret covert ops group called GHOST that will fill the gap between the military and the things they can and can't do and the police and the things they can and can't do. It might mean there are nights I have to be away. But, mostly what it will mean is that families like ours, who are going through what we have been through, will have support at a level like no other. Little red tape, fewer laws holding us back. The waiting was excruciating wondering where you were and what was happening to you especially after your father received the picture; and watching the police slowly collect every piece of evidence and ignoring what we needed to say and our help. In the meantime, you were in the hands of madmen. We can circumvent that and bring family members home sooner."

He kissed her lips. "I need you to know that's what we're planning because it will mean that you'll be home with Emmy alone sometimes. But, I'll always come home to you, Princess and Emmy. I love you."

Her eyes filled with unshed tears again.

"Oh, Dane. That suits you so much better than working in a factory job. I've seen you in action. You're phenomenal in that role; and it's simply perfect."

He hugged her close as his eyes floated to the fireplace and Catherine's picture on the mantle. Her smile as she looked at the camera told him she was smiling on him now. Life was going to be full. Busy. And complete.

Keirnan pulled back. "Dane, we should talk about

something else. Do you want more children? I love Emmy, I do. But, I want more."

He smiled. "How could I not want more children with you as their mother?"

She lunged at him again. And he whispered in her ear. "Besides, making them is so damned much fun."

She laughed out loud and he couldn't help the joy he felt in his heart at that moment.

## 50

"Is it noticeable?"

"No, silly, it isn't. Plus, there's not a soul out there who doesn't know what you've gone through this past month or so."

Lexi was the best. She was always there for her.

Keirnan had been seeing a counselor for a month now; she was fighting to overcome her PTSD and the feeling that everyone will betray her at any moment. It lingered, but she was working through it. Her support system was outstanding.

"Okay, I just want this to be perfect."

Lexi laughed. "Well, I hate to point this out, but we've literally planned a wedding in a month. You're lucky your future mother-in-law can sew, or you'd be wearing jeans and a t-shirt. Zane has gone all out helping you, and for crying out loud, girl, you've got a smoking hot husband and an adorable daughter waiting for you. Who the hell cares if you limp a little?"

She blushed. "I just don't want Dane to think he is

getting damaged goods. Because I feel like damaged goods, Lex."

Her friend came and hugged her.

"Your counselor told you what to do when you have these feelings, right?"

"Yes. Thank you for reminding me. I'm to recite all the good people in my life and why they are still in my life." She patted her hair, which was piled high on her head, curls raining down all around her head. "I have Dane who loves me completely. I have Emmy who started calling me Mommy last week. I have Lexi who is the best friend a girl could have. I have parents and a brother who are always there for me and love me unconditionally. I have a mother-in-law who loves me and sewed me a gorgeous wedding gown made of satin and lace. I have friends at school. None of these people have let me down. Ever. I have financial security. I'm truly blessed. I'm worthy of all of it. "

"There, see? I bet you feel better now."

She laughed, "I do." Then she laughed again, "I'll be saying that again in a few minutes."

The door burst open and Emmy bolted through it with Estella and her mom running behind her.

"She couldn't wait to see you, Keirnan. I hope it's okay."

"Oh, my gosh, of course." She knelt down, which was easier today than yesterday. Her therapy was helping all around. "Come, beautiful; let me hug you my sweet daughter." Emmy sought reassurance often and it relaxed her when Keirnan called her her daughter. When they returned from their honeymoon, she wanted to start legal adoption proceedings to make it official.

Emmy flew into her arms, and hugged her tight.

When she pulled away, she twirled. "Look what Gram made me."

The pretty white dress looked like a miniature wedding dress with a small train that flowed around her. A large bow at the back of the dress set off the whimsy of Emmy so perfectly. Estella captured her personality into a gorgeous dress and Keirnan was so happy to see her joy in wearing it.

"You look beautiful, Emmy. How do you feel?"

"I feel like a Princess. Daddy calls me and you that."

"Yes, he does. Today and every day, he's our handsome prince."

Emmy giggled. "No, he's my daddy."

"Okay, he's my handsome prince and your daddy."

Emmy giggled then turned to Lexi. "Do you like my dress?"

Lexi knelt down and looked Emmy in the eyes. "You look like a dream."

"That's what my other mama said."

Everyone in the room froze.

"Emmy, honey, what do you mean?" she asked. Panic beginning to rise in her chest at the thought that someone else was going to betray her.

"My mama in my dreams. She told me last night that I looked like a dream. You know, my mama in the picture on the fireplace."

Keirnan swallowed the large lump in her throat and held her arms out to Emmy. When her daughter walked into them, she held her close and whispered in her ear.

"Your other mama, Catherine, will always watch over you as your personal angel. Do you know that she loved you more than life?"

"Yes," Emmy whispered back.

"She's always with you, baby. She gave me her blessing to marry your daddy. She's happy with our family."

"I know, she told me that, too," Emmy whispered, then wrapped her arms tighter around Keirnan's neck and held her close.

"Okay, we've got to walk down the aisle in about ten minutes, ladies," her mom said with her cracked voice.

Emmy pulled away, and said, "You look like heaven."

Then she skipped off across the room to Estella whose hand was laying over her heart. Keirnan looked up at her and smiled and Estella blew her a kiss.

Lexi came over to her and handed her the small tiara she'd wear for her nuptials to signify that Dane called her a Princess, and she tucked it up into the curls. When she turned to the women in the room. The women who loved her, her mom, Estella, Emmy and Lexi they all clapped their hands in joy.

"Okay, I need to go and marry my prince."

"Do you Dane, take Keirnan to be your lawfully wedded wife? To have and to hold, from this day forward, for better, for worse, in sickness and in health, till death do you part?"

"I will." His voice was clear and loud and strong.

"Do you Keirnan, take Dane to be your lawfully wedded husband? To have and to hold, from this day forward, for better, for worse, in sickness and in health, till death do you part?"

She smiled at him, his eyes so loving, his smile the brightest she'd ever seen.

"I will." She said as loud as she could. She wanted the

world to hear it. This man was her husband till they died separately or together, however it happened.

"I now pronounce you husband and wife. You may kiss the bride."

Dane pulled her into a loving embrace and kissed her completely. In front of everyone, he tasted her lips. His tongue searched her mouth. His arms embraced her fully and she felt more alive than she'd ever felt in her life.

The cheers from their friends and family rose and she started to giggle. When he pulled away he whispered, "You're mine now."

"Actually, you're mine."

"Hey, that's my sister you're necking with," her brother, Gaige said as he wrapped her in a hug.

"Congratulations, sis. You look so happy."

She held him close, because she'd likely not see him again for a year or so once he went back to the service. Though, when he finished his tour in Bosnia, he was coming to work with Dane and her dad in GHOST because her dad said he needed him.

"I am happy. You need to be happy, too. How is Sophie by the way?"

"Stop. She's Tate's sister."

"So?"

Before he could answer she was pulled away by friends and family wishing her all the best.

## 51

H e walked with his wife to their hotel room and inserted the key card in the security panel. As soon as the light turned green, he held her arm from walking in.

"I have to carry you."

She laughed. "That's supposed to be over the threshold of our home."

"I've decided it's wherever I decide. I've decided it's both here and at home."

"Okay, I'm all for being carried by a handsome man."

He scooped her up and enjoyed the laughter that came from her. Carrying her into the room, he kicked the door closed, then turned and waited while she slid the lock in place, and threw on the deadbolt lock.

Once she finished that, he carried her straight to the bed. Laying her gently on top, he began pulling off his tuxedo. She watched him as he stripped, a saucy smile on her face, her head cocked to the left.

If she wanted a show, he'd give her one. He stepped

back two steps, pulled off his tie and tossed it her way. She threw her head back as she laughed, and he loved the way she looked so much he began unbuttoning his shirt.

Pulling it back from his chest, he wriggled his ass as he scooted his shirt off his arms, twirled it over his head a few times then let it fly over her head.

She clapped her hands and he began unbuttoning his trousers and unzipping his fly as he continued his little dance for her. Shimmying his slacks down his legs he wriggled his hips toward her a few times and earned more clapping.

Stepping from his slacks he then began by tucking his thumbs into his underwear, sliding them down an inch at a time, one side, then the other. Until he was exposed, erect and completely naked before her.

Her laughter stopped, and her mouth took on a sensual lift to her lips as she slowly kicked off her shoes, one then the other. She rolled over to her belly, tossed a saucy look over her shoulder and said, "Hey there, handsome, how about helping me with my zipper?"

He obliged. Kneeling on the bed and slowly lowering the zipper on her gorgeous dress, making sure his hands floated across her body all the way down. Once her zipper was open, his hands slipped inside and caressed her back. Her sexy as hell back, then slid down to her ass and the pretty white lacy panties that barely covered it. Her skin felt silkier than the dress covering her and her ass lifted from the bed as his hands glided over her soft globes.

Gently moving his hands up her back, he softly pushed the material from her shoulders and down her arms. She rolled over and allowed him to pull the material from her body and down to her waist. The shiny material covering her breasts was pretty, but not as much as she was and he tucked his finger under the fabric and lifted it from her body. She smiled at him, reached behind her back and unhooked the offending material. He pulled it from her body and marveled at the beauty of her bared breasts.

"You're a gorgeous woman, Keirnan Copeland and I'm so happy you're mine."

She smiled at him as she shimmied her wedding dress down her hips and legs, then pulled her panties off as well.

"Well, Mr. Copeland, I hope you enjoy making love to a married pregnant woman."

He froze for a second before what she said hit him.

"You're pregnant?"

She giggled. "I found out this morning."

He leaned down and kissed her. His tongue inside of her, his legs wrapped around hers, his body covering hers.

"Keirnan, I'm so fucking happy."

"Me, too, Dane."

Her arms came around his neck as he entered her body, claiming her for the moment and for life. She was his wife. The mother of Emmy and his unborn child. The woman who completed his life. His lifeblood.

Her moans were perfect as he pulled out and entered her again. Her warmth wrapped around him and squeezed him like a glove. Her wetness a tell to how much he did it for her. His body responded to her in every way. Right now, he wanted to pleasure her before his own release, but after this news, it would be nearly impossible not to claim her fully without care of anything. Something primal just wrapped around him and he had to struggle to keep himself in check.

"Yes, Dane, let go," she whispered in his ear.

For fuck sake, how could he control himself when her sweet words egged him on?

"I'm trying to control myself, Princess. But, you need to stop urging me on."

She cried out in his ear, "Oh, Dane." And he felt her pulse as she came.

Pumping in and out a few more times he let himself go and as he fell over the edge, he knew his life was complete.

*＊*

Gaige Vickers is all grown up and running GHOST. The woman he could never forget, Sophie Turner, is now in danger and calling on him for help in:

**Defending Sophie**

**She's the prime murder suspect.**

**He's the man she could never have.**

**Together, on the run and with a murder to solve, sparks fly and passion burns.**

Army sergeant Sophie Turner would do anything for anyone. And after her best friend is murdered, she's hell-bent on uncovering the truth. But when all evidence points to her, Sophie must call the only man she's ever truly wanted for help.

Special agent Gaige Vickers has loved Sophie for as long as he can remember. The second she needs his help, Gaige is there. As they embark upon the truth together, Gaige and Sophie grow closer. Two things are clear: their attraction is undeniable, and Sophie's story doesn't quite add up. Gaige is suddenly torn between his desire for her and his determination to reveal the murderer. But one thing is certain: come Hell or high water, he'll do anything to DEFEND SOPHIE.

. . .

G et your copy of Defending Sophie now.

# ALSO BY PJ FIALA

To see a list of all of my books with the blurbs go to:
https://www.pjfiala.com/bibliography-pj-fiala/

You can find all of my books at https://pjfiala.com/books

**Romantic Suspense**

**Rolling Thunder Series**

Moving to Love, Book 1

Moving to Hope, Book 2

Moving to Forever, Book 3

Moving to Desire, Book 4

Moving to You, Book 5

Moving Home, Book 6

Moving On, Book 7

Rolling Thunder Boxset, Books 1-3

**Military Romantic Suspense**

# ENJOY THIS BOOK? YOU CAN MAKE A BIG DIFFERENCE

Reviews are the most powerful tools in my arsenal when it comes to getting attention for my books. As much as I'd like to, I don't have the financial muscle of a New York publisher. I can't take out full page ads in the newspaper or put posters on the subway.

(Not yet, anyway.)

But I do have something much more powerful and effective than that, and it's something that those big publishers would die to get their hands on.

**A committed and loyal bunch of readers.**

Honest reviews of my books help bring them to the attention of other readers.

If you've enjoyed this book I would be so grateful to you if you could spend just five minutes leaving a review (it can be as short as you like) on the book's vendor page. You can jump right to the page of your choice by clicking below.

Leave your honest review by clicking here.

# MEET PJ

Writing has been a desire my whole life. Once I found the courage to write, life changed for me in the most profound way. Bringing stories to readers that I'd enjoy reading and creating characters that are flawed, but lovable is such a joy.

When not writing, I'm with my family doing something fun. My husband, Gene, and I are bikers and enjoy riding to new locations, meeting new people and generally enjoying this fabulous country we live in.

I come from a family of veterans. My grandfather, father, brother, two sons, and one daughter-in-law are all veterans. Needless to say, I am proud to be an American and proud of the service my amazing family has given.

My online home is https://www.pjfiala.com.
You can connect with me on Facebook at https://www.facebook.com/PJFialaı,
and
Instagram at https://www.Instagram.com/PJFiala.
If you prefer to email, go ahead, I'll respond - pjfiala@pjfiala.com.

Made in the USA
Las Vegas, NV
20 March 2023

69416774R00173